The Γ

D1412797

There once was a boy called Sylvester,' I whisper, 'who had eyes like polished emeralds and white-blond hair, and he was out and about, walking in the sunshine, just walking, minding his own business, and he bumped into this woman with red hair – red signalling nothing – and he didn't really physically bump into this woman, it's just an expression.'

It's a green glitter glue on the light switch. An androgynous colour that no one can complain about. At first I tried chipping it away, but then I got afraid of damaging the plastic and losing my deposit, so I did an internet search about removing glue and one of the things was nail varnish remover. I had some on my dresser which my best friend Patty had left a few months ago, after painting her toenails on my bed with her thighs showing, every shocking-pale inch, and me seeing her red underpants – red signalling nothing, nothing at all – and getting an erection. And it's lucky, her leaving the varnish remover, because I haven't left this room in three days. But that's a whole other story.

'And anyway, he stopped to talk to this woman, and the woman was very beautiful with little fires in her iris and big juicy lips, and he found himself falling madly in love, even though he didn't believe in the concept of love at first sight, and the reason he fell in love so quickly was because she was a witch and she'd done a charm, and she wanted him to fall in love with her because she was feeling insecure and starved of attention this particular day.'

I put some vinyl gloves on. They're important, the gloves. I also have plasters around each of my fingertips. I won't take any risks. I sip my lychee juice and stare at the green-glittered light switch. I am a ridiculous little man, I think. Ridiculous.

'And here's a funny thing about the witch: she had borderline personality disorder, except she'd never been diagnosed, and even if she had she would have dismissed it as hocus-pocus, which is funny, and, anyway, if she *had* been diagnosed and treated, maybe she wouldn't feel the need to go around putting love spells on people just to make herself feel better.'

I sip some more juice. My mouth is dry. I've spent hours gearing myself up for this task. I even thought about asking Keith my housemate to do it, offering him money. A pound a switch. But that would be embarrassing. And I've been avoiding him these last three days. Curled up in my hole like a sick rabbit.

Trying to think clean thoughts.

For a start there were too many people. And that's bad enough. Brown plastic chairs rimmed the walls in a square, and fourteen of them were taken. That's the second bad thing; I have a history with the number fourteen. I don't trust it. It was raining hard outside. I was waiting to see Dr Hunter and I was excited because I like Dr Hunter very much. But there were fourteen people on fourteen chairs. Fifteen people on fourteen chairs if you counted the baby on the woman's lap, and this seemed to highlight the fourteen-ness of the situation all the more. That fifteen, rubbing it in.

An early sign that I should have got out of there, this worrying about numbers.

Some of the people were wet from the rain. This one woman was just wearing a denim jacket over her clothes and it was soaked dark blue. Her drippy-string hair was stuck to the sides of her face and black make-up had spread into her eye wrinkles. I could smell alcohol and cigarette breath coming off her. She was two seats over.

I flicked through some magazines – mostly women's ones and *National Geographic*s dated from last year. I snuck glances at this Indian woman sat opposite me. She had a strange face – perfect eyebrows that sort of swooshed across her forehead, lovely maple syrup eyes, skin like chocolate mousse. Then she had these skinny lips that made me think of bacon rind. When she smiled at the small child next to her, all her gums showed, and they were big gums. Acres of gum. It was odd, this beauty mixed up with ugliness, like a dead bluebottle in a fruit bowl.

She glanced across the room and her maple syrup eyes met mine. Just for a second. What if she could hear my thoughts? What if she just heard all that about the gums and lips?

I tried to swallow the idea back down. No, no. Down the oesophagus in big peristaltic gulps, down, down into the belly, I thought: No, not this again. No. I visualised the idea inside my stomach, remembering GCSE Biology. I saw the hydrochloric acid sloshing all over the idea, breaking it down, I imagined enzymes going at it too, the pepsin, gastrin, mucin. They had tiny turtle faces and they were gnashing at this idea of mine. But it wasn't working. It came back up raw and squirming and awful. It was an idea, an idea with a heartbeat, and soon, in, say, twenty seconds or so, it would be a belief.

It's like my mind is out to get me.

And we're supposed to be on the same side.

I'll tell myself a story, I thought, for distraction. A story. OK. So. There was a fruit fly with green eyes like polished emeralds, and instead of eating its own vomit like other flies, it ate its own earwax … no, that's ridiculous, flies don't have earwax … there was a fly and it had green eyes, and it had green eyes because it was cursed by a witch, and it was also cursed to only be sexually attracted to spiders, which is a horrible curse, a really cruelly ironic curse thought up by a cruel mind, but that was the witch all over, she'd come up with the curse when she was trying to watch her favourite TV program, which was *Dexter*, and there'd been this fly on her TV screen and it wouldn't go away, and it was stopping her from following the narrative, so she did the curse, smiling nastily to herself and dribbling cigarette smoke out of her nose, and this poor fly, it suddenly felt the urge to go and find a spider so it could procreate, and being a tiny-minded thing, it didn't understand that such a thing would be certain suicide, and the thing is … and the thing is…

She was reading my mind right now.

You're reading my mind right now, aren't you?

I started to imagine the Indian woman sucking on a large penis. All close-up and graphic like hardcore pornography. Stringy saliva, foreskin rolled back, slurpy suction noises, lots of gum, a long pink field of gum, and a green-eyed fly crawling up her cheek—

I clenched my eyes shut. I thought: No, Sylvester, not this, you're being *stupid*, you're being—

Then she was getting into the testicles, sort of nuzzling them – they were large and hairy. The penis, which was getting bigger and veinier by the second, was swinging into her face, slapping her cheek, leaving little trails of pre-ejaculate on her skin, and then it crushed the fly which got stuck to the moist surface of the penis head and the woman promptly sucked its squished up body right off like it was a raisin.

I thought, She's not seeing this, she's *not* seeing it, I'm being ridiculous.

But when I opened my eyes she was looking at me. Coolly. Chin tilted. Sliver of gums between her just-parted lips.

My stomach twisted.

She *can*, she can *see* it.

She looked down at her magazine.

I touched my temple. I thought, as loud as possible, I'm sorry, I don't mean to be thinking these things about you, it's just my mind does this when I, when I … oh God…

I was starting to feel faint. My hands were cold. I clenched them, re-clenched them. I could hear a buzzing. A fly? Or just in

4

my head? I sensed eyes on me, looked – it was the alcohol-breath woman in the wet denim jacket. She quickly looked away. Her brow wrinkled. She could read my mind too. The pair of them.

The pair of you.

So now they were scissoring, the Indian woman and the alcohol-breath white woman, both of them naked. They were grinding against each other, hard, like the women in my dad's lesbian films. The old one's breasts were flopping around like half-empty sacks of sugar. She had grey and brown pubes with bits of sick caught up in them. I don't know why there was sick in them. They both had these terrible looks on their faces, like they were disgusted by what they were doing. Like it wasn't their choice to do it. Alcohol Breath squeezed her face up and grunted and eliminated her bowels into one cupped hand, and then she was rubbing the faeces all over the Indian woman's breasts, rubbing it all in, then pushing some into her mouth, spreading it across her gums with a fingertip. And then came a whole swarm of flies, landing on both the women, and still they carried on scissoring and smearing faeces.

My mouth started moving silently. Irrational, irrational, irrational. My heartbeat was going too fast. My hands weren't just cold, they were numb now, and my armpits wet. A bad sign. People were looking at me. Because of the way I was acting – back stiff and straight, skin white and clammy, eyes crazy, chanting silently. Irrational, irrational, irrational. But my broken fuse of a mind didn't see this. This is what it saw: *everyone* in the room could now see my thoughts – the old dignified talcum powder couple in the corner, the fat old man with the walking stick held across his lap, the black man with the restless leg, the pretty girl with the lumpy-faced baby, the almost-pretty girl with the soggy bobble hat and piercings.

There were too many people here. There were children. There were black people.

Niggers, my mind spat. Niggers and Pakis.

5

'Sorry, I'm so sorry,' I said.

I got up fast, almost falling over, and stumbled out of the waiting room, out of the surgery, into the rain. And then I vomited my breakfast into the flower bed. Granola bar and banana all pulped up and watery over some yellow flowers. And then I got home, and I stayed inside my bedroom for three days, ignoring Keith's knocks, and yes, I snuck out in the middle of the night to get some food from the kitchen, but otherwise I was in that room, hiding my thoughts from people, and by the third day I decided to be OK with thinking horrible things, because after all, humans are perverted deep down, and that's fine, that's just biology, so I masturbated a couple of times and I was sort of OK with the content of my fantasies, even though they mostly featured anuses, moist ones, and then I started packing – I was due to move out the next day. And I cleaned the glitter glue from all the switches – the plug sockets, the lights – and I did it with vinyl gloves on and a face like a crumbling tombstone.

Return to the Labyrinth

Dad will be here in half an hour – it's his flat I'm moving into. Back into. When I left last year I didn't think I'd ever go back, never ever, but time heals, like everyone says. I'm at my kitchen table. The hallway in front of me is cluttered with boxes and stuffed bin bags. The radio plays quietly. I always liked this kitchen, even though I never cooked. It's big and airy with pale yellow walls and there isn't as much mould on the ceiling as the other rooms, but the best part is the window, which is massive and has a view of the distant Caerphilly mountains. Right now the skies are clear blue and there are lots of birds like little black Ms gliding around high up.

The reason I'm having to move out is because of Keith. He fell in love with a girl called Esther and now he wants to live with her. She has a nice flat near the city centre. It's got a Juliet balcony. The problem is, if he goes I have to pay all the rent on the house. That's what the landlord says. Either I find a replacement housemate or I pay double. But I haven't found a replacement. And the council won't pay double. It was hard enough getting them to pay for just the single.

Keith comes into the kitchen. He's wearing jersey boxers and he has a bald duvet over his shoulders like a cape. He looks like he's just woken up. There's a splodge of dried blood on the back of his duvet. I wonder if it's Esther's menstrual blood. I wonder what it smells like.

But that's an awful thing to think.

Which is fine. Fine and normal and perverted and human. Fine. I smile at Keith.

He nods a hello and starts making tea for himself. I sit there with my knees pressed together and silently watch him. I like watching Keith make tea. He takes a lot of care. He drags the spoon through the water lazily, and he slowly slowly swirls the teabag around the cup in a way that is almost sensual. I have a problem with spoons – I haven't touched one in over ten years, whole other story – but Keith is so gentle it's almost hypnotic, and this last year I've convinced myself that if I continue to watch him make tea with such love, I can cultivate some positive associations with spoons. He has a system. He lifts the bag to the rim and squeezes it for three seconds (I can see his lips move as he silently counts). He thumbs it into the compost bin. Sinks two perfectly level sugars in, stirs six times, dribbles some milk in, stirs six times. Wipes the spoon with his T-shirt. Puts down the spoon.

You can see the process brings him satisfaction.

He walks back out, then stops at the doorway, turning to me. 'You can have the TV stand if you like.'

'Oh,' I say. 'Thanks.' I don't want the TV stand.

'Esther doesn't like it.'

Keith's toenails are thick and lumpy and yellow. More like scabs than nails. 'Well. Take care.'

I nod and smile. 'You too. I hope you like living in your new house.'

'Flat,' he says.

I nod and smile.

He turns and leaves the kitchen, his duvet dragging dirt and fluff behind him. I watch the menstrual stain shrink to a dot.

Meat. It probably smells like meat.

Dad knocks on the door with his knuckles even though there's a bell. A pair of wraparound sunglasses hide his eyes. I move out of the way and he walks in. His big warm beer belly swipes my arm. He grabs the heaviest binliner, swings it over his shoulder, picks up another and takes them out to his car, frowning. I pick up a small box of books and the guitar I'll never learn to play. I kick a bag of clothes ahead of me.

When we're finished loading, Dad picks a cigarette out of his packet, lights it and leans against the side of his car.

'You wanna say goodbye to your house?'

I shake my head.

'How long were you here for?'

'Almost a year.'

He picks something out of his teeth with his nail. Examines it, flicks it. Looks at me. 'Where's that bike I got you last Christmas?'

'Bike?'

He nods. Takes a drag of his cigarette.

'You didn't get me a bike for Christmas, Dad.'

'Yes I did. Silver Shimano.' He lifts his sunglasses on to his forehead so I can see his eyes. They're hard and blue. 'Where's the bike, Sylvester?'

'You didn't get me a bike.'

'I got you a fucking bike, Sylv. A silver Shimano, twenty-one speed.' He takes a step closer. He's a big man, my dad. 'If you sold it, tell me.'

'You didn't get me a bike, Dad.'

'Just be honest, Sylv. If you sold it or lost it. I don't fucking care. Just be honest.'

'Dad. You didn't get me a bike.'

He lets his shades drop back down. 'What did I get you then?'

'You gave me money.'

His head tilts slightly. 'Did I?'

I nod.

'What about the Christmas before that?'

'Money. You always give me money.'

'You sure?'

I nod. I put my hands in my pockets then take them out again.

Dad blows out smoke. He brings his knuckles to his mouth and stays like that for a while. He looks at me. 'Then who'd I give the bike to?'

I shrug.

He shakes his head. Throws his cigarette onto the ground and opens the car door. 'Come on then.'

I run back inside and leave my keys on the kitchen table. I turn the radio off. There's still green glitter on its switch. Hopefully no one will notice. Dad's got the engine going. I go round the other side and get in. I can smell cannabis. Dad's fiddling with a tiny MP3 player. He's already got another cigarette lit and it's pressed between his lips. Smoke curls up into his face, making him squint. His sunglasses are pushed back into his short silvery hair.

A song comes on. Loud guitars.

'Let's have a bit of Zep,' says Dad, glancing at me, and I smile because I've always told him I like Led Zeppelin, but it's a dishonest smile because really I don't, not particularly, I mean, they're OK, but that's all, and anyway, he does a little nod and shifts the car into gear and we drive off.

I keep my eyes trained on the number plates of the cars in front, making words out of them. SMV– simvastatin. DFE – deferoxamine. POY – pony. NAX – Nasonex. It's a sunny day and the windows are wound right down. When Dad shifts gears his knuckles knock against my knee, so I press my legs together. I don't like to be touched. I mean, sometimes it's OK, like if it's a healthcare professional. Especially Dr Hunter. But other times it gives me the cold belly shivers.

We stop at the lights. Dad keeps his hand idling on the shuddering gear stick, like he's won that bit of territory. His chunky silver watch vibrates on his wrist. I notice how hairy and red-brown his arm is. A dog barks somewhere nearby.

Dad slaps the steering wheel. 'Lenny John!' he says. He looks at me. 'Lenny John I gave the Shimano to.'

Lenny John works in the hospital as a cleaner. My dad knows him because they go to the same café for breakfast every Sunday. But they don't sit at the same table or anything.

'Why did you give Lenny John a bike?'

Dad takes his time answering my question. 'He's done some jobs for me.' He keeps his eyes looking straight ahead.

The lights turn to amber and the car lunges forward.

PRM – paracetamol, CLR – calcipotriol, SUA – salbutamol.

I don't ask what kind of jobs.

Dad lives in a small downstairs flat. I don't know if he has it paid by the DSS or if he pays for it himself. There are two small bedrooms, a small kitchen, a living room and a tiny bathroom that just about fits in an upright shower but no bath. The living room has a large flatscreen screwed to the wall, with tall speakers on either ends of the room for 'proper stereo effect'. There are lots of posters – a *Total Recall* movie poster, a *Rambo* one, an extra large Pink Floyd one (*The Dark Side of the Moon*), a couple of topless women with swollen up, oily breasts, and a black and white still of Jean Claude Van Damme holding out his leg in a sidekick, his foot hovering under a terrified man's chin, from the film *Time Cop*.

The reason he has so many posters is to hide the punch marks in the wall.

Dad keeps the place tidy. He's especially finicky about his coffee table. He wipes it down throughout the day with a cloth he keeps on the magazine rack below. He has coasters, six of them, and if a glass or can or mug goes down without one, he gets angry. He grabs the offending drink, slams it down onto a coaster and stares at the perpetrator, breathing through his nose like a bull.

He has a fruit bowl in the middle of the table which has never held fruit, and this is where he puts his cigarettes, lighter, reading glasses and mobile phone. His remote controls he lines up next to the bowl. He likes them to be parallel to the table edge, and straight, sides not quite touching. Sometimes he'll sit there for ages adjusting them with tiny little finger nudges until he's happy.

Another thing Dad cares about is technology. He likes his appliances to be new and the best quality. But not 'flashy'. As well as *Weed World* he subscribes to two technology magazines – *What Hi-Fi?* and *T3*. Sometimes Dad will talk to me about amplifiers and speakers, and I'll have to pretend to be interested. When he first got a Blu-ray player, he put a James Bond film on and said, 'Look at the quality on that, Sylv,' in this awestruck whispery voice like he was witnessing the aurora borealis, and I didn't have the heart to tell him that it looked the same as usual, and I nodded and said, 'Yes, pretty amazing.'

My bedroom is the same as when I left it. There's a poster of Kate Bush opposite the bed, which I used to look at when masturbating and which I will probably recommence looking at when masturbating. On the other wall, a few photos, including the one of my friend Patty, topless but with spoons over her nipples. There's a chest of drawers, a bare desk and a wardrobe with a large canvas print hidden behind it. I put it there just before I left last year because it caused me some mental disturbance (that's also a whole other story) but I think I'm at a place right now where it won't bother me too much. The buttermilk carpet has been hoovered – I can smell warm static and cooked dust.

I look at the light switch. Clean and white with light scratch marks. I wonder how long he waited after I left last year before scraping the glitter glue off. No nail varnish remover for Dad. A hard spatula or a butter knife. A scrunched-up face.

He dumps the last black bag in the middle of the floor. He laces his hands behind his head and arches his back. His spine crackles. He looks at me.

'I kept it for you.'

'Thank you.'

'In case things went tits up.'

I nod.

'Speggy wanted me to use it as a grow room.' He looks around the room. 'I was tempted. But…' He looks at me. 'Well. I kept it anyway.'

He goes to walk out of the room but stops, turns back. 'No dramatics this time. From either of us.' He looks at a spot near my knee as he says this. 'Fresh start.'

I nod.

He holds out a large finger. '"Don't push it,"' he says, in a gruff American accent. '"Don't push it or I'll give you a war you won't believe."'

It's a line from *Rambo: First Blood*.

'"Can we be frank?"' I reply, also doing the accent, but not so well. '"You're looking terribly anaemic."' This is from *Tango and Cash*. '"I think what you need is a little"' – I cock a pretend gun – '"iron in your diet."' I fire the gun and he clutches his chest like he's been hit.

He smiles and walks out, switching on the light as he leaves.

When Dad talks about dramatics, he means two things: firstly, the time he broke my nose; secondly, the time I took an overdose. Which sounds really bad. Taking an overdose. But it's not actually so bad. I mean, it wasn't a normal, proper overdose like normal, proper teenagers do. Here's what happened.

Dad was watching rugby with some friends/customers. There were five people, including me, crammed into the living room. On the three-seater, Dad and Shaz. Shaz is a plump, middle-aged lesbian with short, bleached-blonde hair. She works in the Spar and gives away all the out-of-date alcohol to homeless people, which is nice, I guess, except she also spends a lot of time saying nasty things about Muslims and Jamaican men. Perched on the armrest was Sudeep, a young Sikh taxi driver who sells cannabis on the side. Then there was Jeff on a fold-up chair. Jeff is a biker with a blond ponytail and big, googly eyes. He smokes a lot of cannabis and goes to biker festivals and has sex with 'bike skanks', which are his words, not mine, because I would never talk about women in that way.

After the rugby was over, Dad went and got his vaporiser from the bedroom. A vaporiser is sort of like a bong, except it turns the cannabis smoke to vapours and is better for the lungs apparently. My dad is very proud of his vaporiser. It's a Verdamper, which is meant to be a good thing, and it's made of glass. 'I'm a Verdamper man,' he likes to say, eyes dancing. Whenever he's nervous or upset about something, he dismantles and cleans it with the care of a soldier cleaning his gun. He has special cleaning equipment. Vera, he calls it.

I went to my room to do a hundred press-ups, because I try to do two hundred every day and hadn't done as many as usual before school that morning as I'd chosen to masturbate twice instead of once, so my routine had been messed up. I came back and Dad was out of the room. His friends/customers were eating wedges of chocolate cake out of their laps. I could see they were taking care with their crumbs.

I sat back down on the floor. Jeff called my name. He was holding out a plate which held five slices of the chocolate cake.

'It's not cannabis cake, is it?' I asked.

Jeff shook his head, jaw working and eyes rolling as he chewed and swallowed. '"Cannabis cake." What's he like? Nah, Shaz brought it along. It's from Spar.'

I took a slice and thanked him. I don't normally eat cake because of all the refined sugar and trans fats, but sometimes I treat myself. I ate it slowly and then licked the crumbs off my hands. I noticed everyone looking at me. 'Sorry, did you say something?'

Jeff looked at Shaz. He was smiling and shaking his head, his ponytail wagging. 'Tell him.'

Shaz smirked. Her eyes were candyfloss pink. 'It *was* hash cake. Sorry – I mean *cannabis* cake.'

They all laughed, except Sudeep, who was looking round the room dopily at people's faces.

I sat there stiffly. Waiting for them to tell me it was a joke. Dad came back in. He looked at me. He looked at his friends/customers. Then back at me. 'What's so fucking funny?' he asked. 'What's going on?'

I just stared up at him. Sweat was beading my temple. He looked down at me quizzically, head tilted.

Jeff stopped laughing. He put his hands on his knees and grinned up at my dad. 'We gave him some cake, din' we? Cept we never told him—'

And Dad lunged at him and grabbed him by his Iron Maiden T-shirt and lifted him up so his stomach hair showed and screamed, 'You fucking what?' in his face.

Silence. Jeff gawped into Dad's face, eyes fluttering. Dad threw him down and he landed on the fold-up chair and it broke under him. He lay sprawled on top of the broken plastic, clutching his lower back.

'You don't give my son drugs, you dopey cunt. They don't agree with him.' He looked at his friends/customers, his eyes skipping from face to face. He signalled for me to stand up and pushed me out of the room. He paused at the doorway and turned back. 'And if that cake is still on the table when I get back, so help me I will murder someone.' And he slammed the door.

He took me to the bathroom and told me to throw up. 'Just stick your fingers down your throat and you'll be fine,' he said. I tried but I couldn't do it. The cake sat inside me in a sickly lump.

Dad looked at me for a long time. I knew what he was thinking. He was thinking that he should force his own fingers down my throat. But he wouldn't. 'Then you're just gonna have to ride it out, son,' he said.

He took me to my room and switched on my PC. He looked through my DVD collection, brought out an old Jackie Chan, put it in my computer's disk drive and put it on.

15

'The thing about getting paranoid when you're stoned,' he said, 'is you've gotta distract yourself. Don't give your brain time to think. Watch films back to back. Action films. Distracting films. OK?'

I nodded. I was scared. The only other time I ever got stoned on cannabis I had a panic attack in the school nurse's office and Dad got called in to take me home. (I'd stolen a spliff from him before leaving for school that morning and smoked it in between coughs in the school toilet because I thought it might calm me down and let me sit in History without worrying about people reading my mind, because isn't that what cannabis is supposed to do, calm people down?) In the car home I'd begged him to take me to the hospital because I thought I was dying – my left arm was going numb, I was going to have a heart attack, I was going to die and not wake up ever again, please, please, please, Dad, I'm going to die – and we'd spent two hours sitting in the waiting room of accident and emergency, me breathing into a paper bag and squinting my eyes shut, him reading the *Daily Mail* from cover to cover and loudly drumming his fingers on his armrest. And by the time the doctor saw me I was all right and Dad kicked a hole in the wall, he was so annoyed, and he ended up having to pay damages to the hospital.

'You'll be fine,' he said now. 'I'll check up on you. It takes a couple of hours when you eat it. You'll probably be asleep by then.'

He looked at me a bit longer and then he walked out and closed the door behind him.

I tried to watch the film. *Drunken Master*. But my hands were going numb and I could see things moving out of the corner of my eyes. The ghosts of all the spiders I'd ever stepped on – that's what my mum used to say that was. I edged up to the far corner of my bed. I felt like there was something in the room with me. That big canvas print I've got shoved behind my wardrobe? Well this was before it got shoved there, before I got obsessed with it, back when it was still on the wall, and I was starting to feel like something was going to come out of it. A long, long skinny arm. A swarm of flies.

There was a boy, I thought, called Sylvester Skillacorn, who had white-blond hair and eyes that shone bright green like emeralds, and the thing about him was he was very small, so small in fact that he slept in a teacup that had belonged to his dead mother. Which she used to drink cocoa out of. Because she loved cocoa. And it was the cocoa that had made her son so small. See, a wicked witch had cursed all her cocoa when she was pregnant, and the more she drank, the smaller the foetus got, and when she finally gave birth to him, she didn't even know it, he was that small, small as a chickpea, but fully developed. And she would have rolled over and squashed him without thinking about it, or else leave him to starve and die or get eaten by cats, except he cried, and even though the cry was like a mouse squeak, she heard it, being a mother with finely-tuned instincts brought about by high levels of oxytocin, and she picked him up and gently laid him on her palm, and naturally she couldn't breastfeed him because her nipple was bigger than his whole body, let alone his mouth, so she, she...

There was definitely something in the room with me.

'Ridiculous,' I whispered, edging closer to the wall, my eyes fixed on the big canvas print. 'Irrational.' My heart was booming. My skin was starting to feel tingly. The cannabis was breaking my thoughts open. I was one of those people too pure for drugs, like Bruce Lee, so the cannabis had started working straight away, sizzling through my bloodstream like rivulets of lava and now it was breaking my thoughts open and inviting faceless spirits with long thin arms into the room, and who knows, I could end up dead, like Bruce Lee.

They say a panic attack can't kill you. I don't believe that for a second.

I went to the bathroom (rushing past the canvas print before

17

it could snatch at me) and looked in the medicine cabinet for Dad's sleeping tablets, which he gets illegally from somewhere. There was a bottle of temazepam. 'Te*mayzee*pam, te*marzee*pam,' I whispered, picking up the box. 'Te*mazzy*pam, tema-zeepalm.' I wasn't sure how many to take because there was no leaflet. I remembered Dad once taking a small handful of them after a party, and he didn't even go to sleep straight away. Just sat in the living room watching *Predator* with sprung-open eyes and a can of lager on his juddering knee. I shook out six of the tablets and took them one by one with handfuls of tap water. I took out two more just in case and swallowed these. I sat on the toilet lid for a long time with my head in my hands. My mind was getting mushy. Swirly. I could hear the tap slowly dripping. I concentrated on this. I made up a story about the dripping. It was cursed by a beautiful, sexy witch to drip all the way down to hell and land on the eyeball of an eternally damned paedophile and thereupon turn with a gasp into steam and rise up before condensing back into drip-form and beginning its redescent into hell, this over and over again. All because the witch was annoyed with the tap for constantly dripping. 'It wasn't even the water's fault,' I remember thinking, before giggling in a sick way. And that's all I remember.

I woke up in a hospital bed. My throat was scratchy-raw. It was from the stomach pumping but I didn't know that then. The melty tablets sucked out. Eight of them. Five milligrams each. Forty milligrams. Probably not enough to kill a cat, I heard later. I had a headache. I sat up and saw my dad. He was in a chair at the end of the bed, reading a magazine. He saw me looking and put it face down on the bed. I wanted to tell him that I wasn't trying to die, that I'd just wanted to knock myself out. But I didn't have to. He knew. He understood. He looked at me with tired, extra-wrinkled eyes. Breathed out a sigh, rubbed his face. Looked at me again.

'You're a fucking nuisance sometimes,' he said.

18

The Sultry Duchess of Ely

After unpacking I go into the living room. Dad is hunched over a magazine on the couch. He's got his reading glasses on – rimless glass, thin metal arms – and his lips are pressed together tight. The TV is on. Some kind of talk show. I sit down on the other side of the settee. He reaches for his cigarette packet in the fruit bowl and taps one out. Lights it, leans back.

A plump woman comes into the room. She has wet hair and she's wearing a fluffy red bathrobe. Red. Signalling nothing. She stops when she sees me. 'You must be Sylvester,' she says.

I nod and do a small smile.

'I'm Delyth.'

I nod again.

She looks at my father. 'You want me to put the chicken on, babes?'

Dad taps his ash into the ashtray on his leg. 'Actually, I was thinking we could go for a meal tonight. The three of us.'

'Oh. OK.' Delyth smiles at me in a way that seems professional. 'Get to know each other, innit?'

I smile back. I can feel my face twitching and wonder if it's visible.

Her eyes go up and down my face and body. She shakes her head. 'You don't look like each other. Not a bit.' And she walks out of the room.

Dad licks his lips. 'She's staying with me,' he says. 'I should've mentioned it.'

'Yes,' I say. 'Maybe you should have.'

Living with a woman, I think. Living with a woman. Then I go over what this means. In practical terms. I will not be able to empty my bowels in this house, ever. The smell-fear, the noise-fear. Sitting there with a sphincter like a frightened bird, listening out with bath-tile ears for the footsteps of other people, ones who will knock and say, 'Oh, sorry,' and then come back when they hear the flush and try not to let on with polite averting eyes that they can smell the faeces through the lavender air freshener. Where am I going to empty my bowels?

Dad's watching me. 'Sorry, I didn't think,' he says. 'She won't be here all day and night. She works.'

I nod and force a smile.

'She used to know your mum,' Dad says. He grinds his cigarette into the ashtray. 'They lived in the same street. Both Ely girls. But your mum was a lot older. Delyth would've been little when I met your mum. Around eight I think.'

He clears his throat and picks up his magazine. I can hear a hairdryer come on in Dad's bedroom. I start to chew on my thumbnail.

'What does she do?'

Dad puts his magazine down. 'She's a beauty therapist.' He lifts a hand, palm out. 'Don't ask.' He shakes his head, smiling happily. It's the first time I've seen him happy-smile in ages. 'You wanna see the crap she's got in my room. All her things. Make-up and … things. I don't know.'

'Maybe she can give me a manicure,' I say.

He just looks at me.

'A joke,' I say, quietly.

He curtly raises his eyebrows, which are like dark moustaches. He doesn't do jokes about men being less than men.

*

20

There's a gap of more than a foot between us on the sofa but I can smell her – almond shampoo and cigarette smoke. That gap between our thighs – it's like a back draft.

Delyth turns to me and smiles.

'So I hear you're named after Sylvester Stallone?'

I nod.

'At least you're not named after Sylvester the Cat, eh?' And she laughs.

'Yeah, I guess.'

She pulls a cushion out from behind her and places it on her stomach. Folds her hands over it. 'Why Sylvester Stallone then?'

I hesitate. The truth is that my dad used to be a heroin addict, before I was born. And during cold turkey he watched a lot of action films. He said it helped him. He still watches action films when he feels stressed. For distraction. It makes me wonder how busy his mind is. It makes me think that his mind is a little like mine.

I easily could have been an Arnold or a Bruce, but the *Rambo* films were his favourite. 'Sylvester Stallone helped me kick smack,' he likes to joke to his friends. But he's only half-joking.

'He just really likes Sylvester Stallone,' I say.

She nods with her mouth open.

'He has a high IQ apparently,' I say.

'Really?'

'Hundred and sixty.'

'Wow.' She smiles. 'He don't look too clever, mind.'

Dad opens the bedroom door and pokes his head out. 'Where's my weighing scales, Del?'

Delyth shrugs. 'I dunno. Where you left them.'

He frowns and withdraws his head.

Delyth picks up the remote control and starts flicking through the channels. Her nails are long and painted. Her hands are small. I imagine them wrapped around a thick penis, pumping like a milkmaid.

Careful, Sylvester.

The bedroom door opens and Dad and Sudeep come out. Dad is folding a couple of banknotes in half. He slides them into his front pocket and pats Sudeep on the shoulder.

'You stickin' around for five?'

'Yeah, sure,' says Sudeep. He sits on the floor and gets his cigarette papers out. He's got a burgundy turban on today and a leather jacket. 'Put the kettle on, Sylv, there's a good boy.'

I stare at him.

'Four sugars,' he says.

I look at Dad. His eyes meet mine and an understanding passes between us like ultrasound. 'I'll do it,' he says.

I started on light switches. Four years old, stood on a stool. I had to run my fingertip along every bit of the light switch – the edges, the corners, the button – in a particular order and pattern. But just once was never enough. My fingertip would do the pattern, and then I would strongly feel like I needed to do it again. Like I hadn't satisfied … something. Like I hadn't got it just right. It was a feeling as powerful as nausea or anger or fear or hunger. An itchy feeling. If I didn't get it just right, maybe bad things would happen. To Mum, to Dad. Unnameable bad things. So I had to start the pattern all over again. Being made to stop early is like when you're drifting off to sleep, almost there, and you're suddenly woken up by a gunshot in the street outside. Which is something I've never experienced, living in Britain, but it's the best example I can think of.

It's not just light switches.

When I was five I started doing a similar thing with spoons. I'd scrape the edge of the spoon along the inside surface of the bowl I was eating out of. Patterns like spirals or figure eights or wobbly jags. The pattern was important – central in fact. It signified something. It was where the magic came from. Like a code from God. I could be sitting there for half an hour gently scraping away at my Kellogg's cereal bowl over and over again, my mum watching me nervously, my dad gritting his teeth. Over and over again. Slowly, slowly. Under a spell. Not being able to stop because I didn't feel like I'd got it *just right* yet. And sometimes Dad would lose it and snatch the spoon out of my hand and shout, 'Stop it, fucking stop it!' And these times I would cry so hard I'd hyperventilate, and Mum would shout at Dad, call him an animal, and he'd punch a hole in the door and storm out of the house with a face made of razor blades and thorns.

OCD wasn't such a well-known thing back then. You'd get the odd segment on morning television about people who washed their hands a hundred times a day, but there hadn't been a film made about it. Mum did her best. No more cereal in the mornings. Toast or a Tracker bar. In school I had packed lunches. No lunchbox, just a sandwich wrapped in cling film, a Wagon Wheel, and some fruit in a carrier bag.

Knives and forks are OK, chopsticks are OK. I must have made some abstract decision when I was small that only spoons stop bad things, though I don't remember. The magic is in the rules. In the code. You'd think I'd be OK with glasses and mugs and bottles, because there aren't many patterns you can make with a circular rim. Except there are, if you're inventive. So I stick to cartons, or I use a plastic beaker that I've cut little jags and grooves into which irritate my finger if I try anything. It makes me feel like a child, having my own special beaker. Like a stupid little boy.

I tried all sorts of things to deal with the light switch problem. None of them worked, except for the glitter glue. I need smooth surfaces, see, as well as smooth naked fingers. When Mum was alive she wanted to get me some of those lights that you activate by clapping, like you see in American sitcoms, but Dad wouldn't have it, because he thought it would indulge the OCD, and that the only way to deal with it was by forcing me to face my anxieties, which some counsellors and specialists agree with – exposure therapy. But that's not why he thinks this way.

'Your father is very much schooled in the "pull your finger out and pull your socks up and get over it" academy,' my mum used to say. 'He's a man's man.'

He didn't like the glitter idea. It took Mum weeks to get him to agree to it, and after it was done, he looked at the glitter – blue, he made sure it was blue – all over my switches and my mouse pad and my keyboard, he looked at it with his stubbly smirk, the way he looks at gay men in the street, and he muttered, 'Ridiculous, just ridiculous,' and Mum gave him a dirty look and said, 'It's not your bedroom, you don't have to like it, Carl.' And that was that.

There are other things I avoid. Certain jewellery, clean ashtrays, plug sockets, certain tablet foil packs, watches, picture frames and lots of electronic switches/buttons. I avoid them like the devil.

Sometimes just looking at a light switch makes me feel sick with woolly-bellied associations.

You could say that light switches are my kryptonite.

I worry that it will get worse. That it will spread to tables, fingernails, book covers.

Skin.

That I will waste most of my life slowly tracing surfaces with my fingertip in a rolling-eyed stupor. Me with a long, blond beard, skinny and sun-starved, dragging my quaking finger around a window frame in a bright-lit room on a dark night.

Then there's blinking.

But that's a whole other story.

Dad got angry with the chopsticks like he always does. He's eating his lemon chicken with a fork now. Delyth keeps glancing my way. I chew very slowly and neatly.

We're near a corner, by the window. There aren't too many people here. Dad gets the attention of a nearby waiter with a look. He lifts up his almost empty drink and the waiter nods. 'Get her another rosé, too,' he says, gesturing to Delyth. He looks at me, eyes darting to my special beaker, which shames him horribly and which Delyth has so far been too polite to ask about. 'You?'

'I'm fine, thank you.'

'Listen to the manners on that,' says Delyth, smiling. 'Doesn't get it from you, does he, Carl?'

Dad drops his fork onto his plate, leans back, burps, and wipes his mouth with a napkin. 'Who needs manners when you've got money?' He stands up, leans down and kisses the top of Delyth's head. 'Going for a piss.'

She glances at me. I put down my chopsticks because nerves have suddenly stolen my hunger. She takes a sip of her wine then holds the glass in both hands, her elbows on the table. I can see her cleavage. Soft as raw bread dough. She's got a heart-shaped face. Prominently. I mean, you look at her face and straight away you think 'heart-shaped'. She's got crow-black hair that flicks out in layers with some bits curling around her face. Large, dark eyes, thinly plucked eyebrows, tanned skin. Really, the best way to describe her is to say that she looks like Christina Ricci if Christina Ricci hadn't been brought up with a personal trainer and a dietician.

'So how old are you, Sylvester?'

'Eighteen.'

'Really? I thought you were younger. You seem … I dunno. Innocent. No offence. Not in a bad way.' She stares at me. 'You really don't look anything like your father. You're so much… D'you bleach?'

'Pardon?'

'Do you bleach your hair?'

I shake my head.

'That's your natural colour?'

'Yes.'

'It's lovely. So light. Like whassis-name – the Milkybar Kid.'

'Uh. Thank you.' I sip my juice. There's a long taut silence that makes the space behind my ribcage feel like an old attic, and then

25

the waiter comes over with a fresh glass of wine and a bottle of beer and a clean glass. Delyth nods her thanks. She drains her previous glass and passes it to him. Puts her elbows back on the table and looks at me.

'How come you don't drink then?'

'I don't like it.'

'What? The taste or the effect?'

'Both.'

Delyth raises her eyebrows. 'Fair enough.' She tucks her chin in and suppresses a burp. 'Carl tells me you're unemployed. You looking for anything?'

'Yes,' I lie. I don't want to tell her I'm on incapacity benefit.

'So what would your ideal job be?'

'Pharmacist.'

She smiles wryly. 'Kind of like your father.'

I mirror her smile. 'Yes.'

'Why? If you don't mind me asking…'

'Um. I like tablets I guess. You know? How they come in different shapes and colours and stuff. Like precious gems or something…' I glance away embarrassed because I'm like a small child with my dumb wonder and my special beaker. The Milkybar Kid. 'I don't take drugs or anything,' I add.

'None of my business if you do,' she says.

My favourite thing about a tablet is its name. Omeprazole, Plenaxis, paroxetine, qualaquin, ziconotide, alfacalcidol. Like poetry. Like an alien language.

Alien poetry.

My favourite name is diclofenac. I don't know why – I mean, if we're talking about how a word feels coming out of your mouth, alfacalcidol is clearly the best word. The clear, clicky kays contrasting with the lull of the ells, the soft dee. But diclofenac has more depth to it – more levels. I love how it can be pronounced in lots of different ways, depending on which parts of the word you emphasise and how you say the vowels. Diclo*fen*ac. Di*clof*enac. A

26

hard F, or F like a V, like in the Welsh language – diclov-enac. Or *clov* like clove – diclove-enac. *Di* like die or dee, or *di* like the *di* in diplodocus. And other languages have other rules, which bring in even more variations. When I'm anxious I sometimes pick the name of a drug and find as many ways to pronounce it as possible.

Of course, I don't tell Delyth any of this. Instead I listen to her talk about beauty therapy. 'We even do some holistic stuff,' she says, running the tip of her pearly fingernail up and down the stem of her wineglass.

Dad comes back. He looks around the restaurant for a waiter or waitress, doesn't find one, turns back to us.

'So, we having afters or what?' he asks us. And he finally gets the attention of a small, beautiful waitress, who brings over the coffee and dessert menu, but there is only ice cream available, as usual, and it comes in a bowl. With a spoon.

'Eat it with a fork, you daft get,' says Dad, grinning. 'Just do it fast before it starts melting.'

Delyth looks at him confused because she doesn't understand the spoon business, he hasn't told her, and he smirks down into his menu, but the grin has fallen off and a muddy mixture of defiant embarrassment is clutching at his eyes, and of *course* he hasn't told her about the spoon business.

On the way home I avoid the cracks in the pavement. It's awful, me doing this, because it's not OCD, it's me hoping that Dad notices and *thinks* it's OCD. A new strain of the virus. I shouldn't be so passive aggressive. That's what counsellors have said in the past, because 'it's a type of avoidance that is detrimental to relationships' and I would do myself a lot of favours if only I could 'convey my feelings directly'. But then, Dad shouldn't tease me.

Anyway, he doesn't notice.

When we reach the front gate, Dad turns to look at next door's house. There's movement in the window – part of a face and a hand – and then the golden curtain is flickering.

'What are you looking at?' shouts Dad.

Delyth puts her hand on Dad's arm. 'Carl. Don't bother.'

Dad glares at the window, mouth a slit. He looks at Delyth. 'Always at that window,' he says. 'Curtain twitching prick.' He opens the gate, exhaling through his nose.

Me and Dad moved into this flat four years ago when I was fourteen, just after Mum died. He threw a flat-warming party. Around thirty people came and crammed themselves in, half of them spilling out into the back garden. Dad invited the people in the flat upstairs – a couple of students – and they quickly became new friends/customers. Emboldened by this, and the beer, Dad went next door to meet his new neighbour on the left. Aled Mellor answered the door. They looked at each other. And Dad saw that he'd made a mistake.

Aled Mellor is a retired office-type person. He has an unusually large skull and a low, straight hairline. Like a light bulb in a badly fitted wig. He has a fat, lumpy nose and he wears square glasses. He has broad shoulders and a stomach like my dad's – solidly fat, not jiggly fat.

The most interesting thing about Aled is his left hand – it's shrunken and warped. His fingers look like they've been melted away like candlewax held close to fire. His pinky is the size of a jelly bean.

Dad gruffly introduced himself and offered Aled a bottle of beer. Aled shook his head like it was out of the question. 'All I want from you,' Aled said, 'is to turn that music down.'

Dad walked away without saying a word.

'Some people are trying to sleep,' Aled said to his back.

Dad just kept walking.

'If he was trying to fucking sleep,' said Dad, back at the flat, 'why wasn't he in his 'jamas? And it's not like we're blasting fucking techno or anything. It's a nice atmosphere.' He tapped Sudeep's arm and said, 'Ask me who I am.' Sudeep looked at him with bleary confusion. 'Just ask me who I am,' my dad repeated. 'Who are you?' said Sudeep. Dad pretended to shoot a shotgun at him and said, in his best Arnold Schwarzenegger voice, '"I'm da pardy pooper,"' which is a line from *Kindergarten Cop*. Everyone laughed and Dad turned the music up a couple of decibels. 'Show the bastard.'

Aled was at the door ten minutes later channelling his grey conservatism into a screwy brow. He looked Dad in the eye and said, 'Turn. It. Down.' – like he was speaking to a naughty child. 'I'm calling the police next time. That's a promise.' Then he walked away.

'Hey!' Dad called, and you could see Aled's shoulders drop with a sigh. As if this naughty child couldn't get any more bothersome.

'What?' he said, turning around wearily.

'"You should clone yourself."'

'*What?*'

'I said you should clone yourself.'

'What are you bloody talking about?' Aled's face was full of disgust. 'Why on earth should I do that?'

Dad smirked and said, doing Schwarzenegger again, '"So you can go and fuck yourself."' (*The 6th Day*).

Aled wasn't to be so easily baited. He held up a finger (from his good hand) and jabbed it in the direction of Dad's face. 'Turn it down. *Now.*'

Dad isn't the sort of man who can afford visits from the authorities. He turned off the song and fell onto the sofa in a drunken sulk, muttering 'k' words like *fuck* and *cock* and *prick* under his breath and slowly turning his beer can into an hourglass.

He put three holes in his bedroom door.

The atmosphere wasn't so nice anymore.

After the party, Dad snuck outside and poured bleach over Aled's flower beds. Since then, Dad and Aled have been at war. Here are some of the things that Dad has done to Aled:

Urinated through the letterbox.

Called his wife a 'useless twat'.

Spray-painted 'Jeremy Beadle Hand Bastard' in spiky red writing across his car bonnet.

Threatened to break every bone in his body.

Dad isn't proud of his actions. They're things he's done when drunk. He regrets every one, except for the threat of violence, because he sees that as honest and open and true. He doesn't enjoy sneaking around by starlight with Domestos tucked under his armpit.

Here's what Aled has done to Dad:

Petitioned to have him evicted.

Reported him to the police twenty-two times.

Called him an ignorant thug.

Stolen his mail.

That's all so far. Mostly the allegations Aled has made to the police concern loud noise or vandalised property. Other neighbours tell the police that Dad's volume levels are OK. The police see Aled Mellor as a nuisance and a busybody. An incessant complainer. They don't take him seriously. Nor does Dad. But he hates him anyway. He hates his angry-pie face and his tiny melted hand. His gold taffeta curtains. I'm not sure Aled's so harmless. If he ever found out what really goes on in Dad's flat – I don't know. I try not to think about it. Diclo*fen*ac.

Dad is so worked up about the 'curtain-twitching wanker' next door that he forgets to keep the hall and bathroom lights switched on for me and I don't want to remind him in front of Delyth. I urinate in the dark. I think I get some on the seat. Dad won't like that. Next time I'll sit down to go, like a girl. He won't like that either.

I read fifteen pages of my book. I do some exercises – a hundred press-ups, fifty sit-ups, fifty squats. I brush my teeth for two minutes and get into bed. I lie awake for a long time. It doesn't get quiet until near midnight, which is when Dad 'closes up shop' on a weekday.

I start feeling sleepy. Then I hear banging next door. In Dad's bedroom. And moaning – a woman's moaning.

My penis is pushing up against the duvet like a nervous mouse under a rug. I tell myself it's OK. You're not weird. You're aroused because you can hear a female having sex. It's perfectly understandable. It's science.

I start to masturbate. I use an old fantasy – eighties Kate Bush with glossy red lipstick performing oral sex on me. Because she has these large pillowy lips and I like the idea of the lipstick getting smeared all over me. Sometimes my mind switches to images of Delyth's wet, twitching anus and I force it to switch back, because though it's biologically acceptable to be aroused by a woman's sex noises, what has her anus got to do with it?

Right at the end I just give up trying.

The Good Witch of Alfacalcidol

I have an appointment with Dr Hunter today – the appointment I should have had four days ago. I like her more than any other doctor. She's friendly but in a professional way, cool and warm at the same time, like a test tube filled up with melted chocolate. She doesn't smile much, but when she does, it's beautiful. When I describe my problems to her she listens one hundred per cent. She has straight black hair in the Japanese style, but she's not Japanese. Her eyes are treacle-black, her skin pale. She has a very symmetrical face, which apparently signifies attractiveness. She doesn't wear make-up – she doesn't need to – but I bet if she wore red lipstick she'd knock everyone out. Dr Hunter's first name is Sheila, which is awful. I never think of her as Sheila. I'm in denial about it.

I need some diclofenac. It's the only drug I've ever been prescribed, apart from amoxycillin for tonsillitis. Doctors have tried to give me all sorts of tablets over the years. Mind tablets, for OCD, anxiety, other things too probably. I've always resisted. I don't want to be on drugs that make changes to how my brain works. I don't think this is unreasonable of me.

I've had a tense neck and shoulders for a long time. My trapezius muscles are full of knots. Diclofenac is a non-steroidal anti-inflammatory analgesic. It helps a little. Though sometimes nothing helps and my upper back feels like the gnarled bough of an old tree.

Trapezius is a great name for a muscle I think.

I have this fantasy that goes like this: I'm out in the woods at night and a UFO comes down, filling the clearing with bright white light and swirling leaves. Some aliens come out and take me up into their spacecraft. They're typical aliens – glowing, bald craniums, black beetle-shell eyes. I could probably make them more original but that isn't the point of the fantasy. They take my clothes off, lie me down on a metal table and do tests on my body. The same kind of tests a doctor does, but for longer. I like it when doctors do their tests – it gives me this fuzzy feeling inside as if my lungs are being whispered to.

Sometimes, when I'm masturbating, Kate Bush has a stethoscope and a rectal thermometer.

Anyway. When the aliens are finished, they say, telepathically, 'Thank you for co-operating. We have learnt a lot from you. Is there anything we can do in return?' And I say, 'Well, I do have this tenseness in my trapezius muscles.' And they say, 'We have just the thing.' They bring out this device – a rod with a ruby-red glowing bulb on the end. They hover the wand over my neck and shoulders and upper back, transmitting some kind of extraterrestrial frequency, and my muscles immediately relax and unknot. My long sloping trapezii become as smooth as a tongue. I feel brand new.

The aliens also make my penis longer and cure my brain of OCD and add two stone of pure muscle to my wiry-lean body and correct the breakage bump in my nose from when my dad punched me last year. Sometimes, I make it so the aliens give me superpowers – telekinesis or indestructibility.

The waiting room is half-full. I go to the receptionist's desk and tell the woman that I need to wait outside, so can she please call me when it's my turn? She looks at me funny and I can tell she's going to say no, that all patients must wait in the waiting room and what makes me so special, so I lean in and whisper, 'I have anxiety,' and her harsh stare vanishes in a finger click and she agrees, nodding with concerned eyebrows. But she's not really concerned, I don't think, she's just scared of getting into trouble.

When I finally see Dr Hunter she's sitting behind her desk in a short-sleeved white blouse. Her arms are long and the colour of vanilla Mini Milks. They have moles on them, maybe a dozen. She's got glasses on today, the sort with thick black frames.

'Hello, Sylvester,' she says. 'How can I help?'

I sit down, back straight, and place my hands on my squeezed-together knees. 'Hello, Dr Hunter. Can I have some more diclofenac please?'

I stress the 'fen' and I say the f as an f.

Dr Hunter nods. She turns to her computer and starts typing. 'They're still helping then?'

'Yes.'

'Not having any stomach pains?'

'No.'

She prints out a prescription and hands it over. She looks at me. 'How's the touching? The, uh, compulsion?'

I shrug. 'Sort of under control. For the moment.'

'I heard you had to rush out of the waiting room the other day …?' She arches her eyebrow ever so slightly.

'I had a funny moment.'

'OK…' She nods to herself. 'Have you thought anymore about CBT?'

I shake my head like a child offered sprouts. CBT stands for cognitive behavioural therapy. It's meant to be very good for all sorts of things, such as drug abuse and anxiety and eating disorders. I've had various counsellors and therapists over the years (my first at age nine) and though it's been nice to talk to them (most of them), I've never made much headway. Meaning my inner life is still a massive headache. My friend Patty says CBT has helped with her OCD. I tried it once – I was on the waiting list for a year. Finally I got an appointment. It was with a man called Dr Thornton. He was skinny with a very prominent skull, like Aled Mellor next door, and a strong Yorkshire accent. He told me to sit down instead of offering. 'Sit.' Like that. I got a bad feeling. There was something about his eyes that reminded me of snake eyes, but I couldn't figure out what it was. They were the pale creamy blue of certain marbles I'd owned as a child. The pupils were kind of normal. Maybe a little misshapen. That was probably what it was. Subtle.

Dr Thornton spent the next five minutes talking to me like I was stupid. He told me that CBT was a very direct therapeutical approach and that, 'essentially', I'd have to do as I was told. He laced his fingers together and leaned forward, elbows on desk, and looked at me for a long time with his snake eyes and I imagined that his super-size cranium was pulsing like he'd spilled radioactive waste on it once, in the 1950s, and then I wondered if maybe all people with large skulls were mean and humourless and then he sighed through his nose like he was depressed at the sight of me. He made me so angry I stopped being nervous for once. I stood up and said, 'You're a very rude man, Dr Thornton,' and I walked out on weak legs and never went back.

Dr Hunter had been very shocked when I'd told her about Dr Thornton. She said that when you're dealing with people who have problems which require CBT, you must have good people skills and definitely a good portion of empathy, and this Dr Thornton sounded like he had none at all. She didn't understand how he hadn't lost his job ages ago. I'd said, 'Well, not all doctors are nice like you,' and she'd given me one of her rare smiles and I'd blushed. She told me I should try CBT again, that it was very unlikely I'd have Dr Thornton a second time; she would even see to it that I didn't, and, in fact, she would make a formal complaint on my behalf if I liked. But I got very anxious when I thought about it.

'Well, you just tell me when you're ready,' she says now. 'If you ever are.'

I nod.

She leans back in her chair, picks up her pen, and starts tapping her knee with it. 'I saw you the other day. You were walking past my house. It was cloudy and drizzly but you were wearing sunglasses.'

'Sometimes I don't like it when people can see my eyes,' I say.

She nods. 'You looked like you were in a bubble. I think you had earphones on as well. And then you went into a health food shop. Which I approve of, of course.'

I smile an earnest smile. All my smiles for Dr Hunter are earnest.

She shifts around on her seat. Lifts her perfect eyebrows. 'Anything else, Sylvester?'

Normally I'd ask her to take my blood pressure and check my pulse. I do this sometimes. I make it look like I'm being neurotic, but really I just like it when she touches me. Today I'm distracted. I'm thinking about what Dr Hunter has just said: I was walking past her house. And then I went into a health food shop.

I know where she lives.

'Um. No, thanks,' I say. I lift up the pale green prescription and look at it. I hope it's not a repeat prescription. I don't want to wait three months until I see Dr Hunter again. I turn the script over. A single prescription for twenty-eight tablets. Good. I can see her again in twenty-eight days, sixteen if I want.

She nods. 'Take care.'

I stand up, tell her thank you, and walk out.

Wellfield Road, I think. She lives on Wellfield Road.

I take this thought home with me and play with it like an old and curious toy.

Predator

Masturbate, exercise, shower, dress, breakfast, juice – this is how I start every morning. If I don't, the day will turn out badly for me. The worst thing is just staying home in pyjamas. It's like a bear trap around the ankle, crunching into bone. I get mentally stuck and I feel dirty and it's just masturbate, Minesweeper, masturbate, Minesweeper, all day long.

Today I'm going to read in the sunshine.

The garden is small and scruffy. Dad shares it with the students upstairs but they never come down. On either side of the garden are wooden fences which come up to nipple height. Aled Mellor's garden is very neat and well kept with flower baskets and gnomes. There's an ornamental well. Dad defecated into it once.

I'm reading Paulo Coelho's *Veronika Decides to Die*, which is sad and sexy at the same time. But I'm having trouble taking it in. I keep thinking of Dr Hunter. I run over my appointment with her, everything she said. It occurs to me that it was very unprofessional, her hinting at where she lived like that. Doctors aren't supposed to do that. There are boundaries. I remember times when I've passed doctors on the street and they've avoided my glance, looking uncomfortable, maybe even a little nervous, because they don't want the fourth wall to collapse. So it was strange of Dr Hunter, talking to me the way she had. Boundaryless. I wonder if she was being careless or maverick or if she wants me to know her address, wants me to work it out. And always giving me prescriptions for only one month – never a repeat for three months, which would make more sense. Because they're only anti-inflammatories, diclofenac, not antidepressants or antipsychotics or newish drugs that need checking up on. And I've tolerated them well for years. Yet always a script for twenty-eight tablets. As if she wants me back to ask for more…

This is dangerous thinking. So I stop and instead imagine what Dr Hunter looks like in everyday life doing everyday things. In a T-shirt, making a sandwich. I think of her pale Mini Milk arms with the moles and her slender fingers around the refrigerator handle. But my mind plays a dirty trick on me and I'm seeing Delyth splayed out on a bed with her plump legs spread out like an M and her vagina a red slit inside a thick black nest of hair, and she's got a pencil inserted into her anus with just the nib poking out and lubricant is dribbling out like warm coconut oil.

Dad comes out clutching a mug. I quickly drop my book on my lap. He drags the other chair into the sunlight, next to me, and sits down. His face is sweaty. He sips his drink and squints up at the whipped blue sky. 'Your mum used to like sitting in the garden,' he says.

'Yeah?'

He nods. 'She loved sunlight. She always said her happiness was solar-powered.'

'I didn't know that,' I say.

'No?'

I shake my head.

'Must've been earlier on,' he says. 'She didn't have so much time to soak up the sun later.'

'Because of me?'

'Well, yeah. Children take up a lot of time.' He glances at me. 'All children do.' He lights a cigarette and continues looking at the sky. 'Course, there weren't grandparents around to help us out. And I probably wasn't as helpful as I could have been.'

Mum's parents had died when she was quite young, her father

of a heart attack and her mother, just two days later, of a brain embolism that made her drop dead in her tracks, right in the middle of ordering flowers for her husband's funeral. And then Mum's little brother died literally two days later, of a severe case of pneumonia, so her whole family, with the exception of her nan, granddad and older sister, were wiped out in one week, which is just horrific. Dad's dad, who was apparently a real nasty piece of work – 'very hands with his fists' – had died of hypothermia after passing out drunk one night on his allotment patch while it was snowing. 'Good riddance to the cunt,' Dad always says when he tells people about this. His mother, a saint apparently, 'who wouldn't say boo to a goose', died when I was five, of cervical cancer, and I still have memories of her giving me pear drops and talking Welsh at me and covering my face with kisses.

'Did great-nanna and -granddad ever help?' I ask.

'Your great-granddad did sometimes, when he was up to it. He used to take you to Barry Island. But then they took his licence off him because his eye sight was going and he refused to wear glasses, the stubborn old git. He used to bomb through the streets of Swansea like a fucking racer boy, it was a miracle he never killed anyone. Your great-nan was too frail. And too busy telling everyone how to live their life.' He shakes his head. 'She was a piece of work.' There's a rustling noise. Dad sits up straight and looks around for the source. The rustling comes again. He hits me on the arm and nods his head toward Aled Mellor's fence. 'He's fucking eavesdropping,' he whispers.

He hands me his cigarette to hold and stands up. He walks silently and crouchingly toward the fence. He reaches it and peers over the top. Then he quickly retreats. 'It's the wife,' he whispers, taking the cigarette from my fingers. 'She's weeding.'

He looks disappointed.

I walk fast, clenching my sphincter and sweating. I get to the Hog and Goose and walk inside. It's an old man's pub. Almost empty.

Dark, quiet, cool. I head to the toilet and check the cubicles. Empty. I run into the furthest cubicle, unbutton my trousers and collapse onto the toilet. It's immediate.

I go to the bar and ask for a lemonade. The barman says two pound. Two pounds, I think. Two pounds is what I'll be paying to empty my bowels every day from now on. Fourteen pounds a week. I go back to my table and pour the drink into my special beaker.

Since I'm out of the house with a whole day to burn, I decide to go for a walk. Just let my feet take me somewhere. But that isn't what happens. My subconscious is steering me, not my feet.

It's taking me to the health food shop.

That's a bad thing – that's what stalkers do. I'm not a stalker. I mean, I've never even masturbated over her. I wouldn't. I'll just go in the health food shop because I'm actually in need of some things, genuinely I am, and maybe I'll see her house and that's OK.

The reason I've never masturbated over Dr Hunter is because she's special. Pure.

I get to Pulse 'n' Grain, the health food shop, and have a look around me. There are shops on both sides of the road. There's also a small cluster of terraced houses wedged between Pulse 'n' Grain and the Cardamom Tree. The houses are numbered 113, 115, 117 and 119. They all look the same – white with blinds in the bay windows and varnished front doors. All joined flank to flank.

I go in Pulse 'n' Grain and buy some fruit and nut bars and flapjacks and some mixed seeds and a Jazz apple, which are my favourite because they're the crispiest, and a bag of crisps made out of plantain or cassava or something like that. You see, I actually needed to buy some things.

There's a tiny park on the side opposite Pulse 'n' Grain. It's a diamond-shaped patch of grass criss-crossed with gravel paths, surrounded by some hedges and black spiky railings, which always make me think of suffragettes or grisly skewery death or Victorian orphans. It has two benches. I go into the park and sit on the bench nearest the railings. I can see the cluster of houses.

The houses she wanted me to know about?

Careful.

I eat a Jazz apple. I try to look at the houses from the side of my eye. A lot of people walk past. I look at the spiky railings and imagine falling on them from a great height. The spikes going through cartilage and eye sockets and internal organs. Through testicles. Knee caps. Being stuck there for hours, dying slowly. I glance at the houses again. I imagine the windows as eyes. Them watching me as I watch them. Quietly amused, with the personalities of old, Oxford-educated white men smoking pipes.

I've been sat here for half an hour.

I realise I'm being weird – bad-weird – and I go home.

The Boy Who Bought Jelly Tots

Patty is my only friend, if I'm being honest. I met her a few years ago at group counselling for young nutcases, which wasn't its official name but it might as well have been. Patty has this form of OCD where she has to count things in groups of seven. Which is interesting because two sevens equal fourteen. Also, when she was very young, every time she saw an ice cream van in the street, she would run home and take a shower. She's never told me why. Also, she had a mental breakdown when she was twelve because she was convinced her bones were growing into spears and that they would end up splitting out of her skin and keep growing until she was a dead, pierced, thorny thing. Which was why she had to count everything in sevens – to stop this from happening. This is called magical thinking. Which sounds a lot sparklier than it really is. My type of OCD is magical thinking mixed up with touching and intrusive thoughts. And maybe other things, undiagnosed things, which I'd rather not think about. Anyway, Patty had it bad and she was institutionalised and pumped full of drugs and she missed school for a year, and now she's OK, she has her CBT and it helps, but she drinks a lot and has sex with different people every week. I like Patty very much because she's honest. Except about her name. It isn't Patty, it's Sarah, but she thinks Sarah is boring.

Patty likes me, she says, because I am all innocence on the outside but inside I'm 'perverted as fuck'. Like Baby Herman from

Who Framed Roger Rabbit. Also she thinks I'm 'outrageously self-aware' for someone so young, which she thinks is a result of all the therapy I've had. I guess I am quite self-aware, and though I'm glad it's been noted, it can be a real burden sometimes. Like when I do something nice for someone, telling taxi drivers to keep the change, returning lost wallets to their owners, stuff like that, and instead of just enjoying the feeling of being nice, I immediately question my motives and conclude that I only did that nice thing to make people think I'm a good person or to gain their approval.

Patty is chubby but not obese. She has dyed black hair with a straight fringe. Kind of like Dr Hunter's, but not so Japanese – more burlesque. I can tell this because the fringe sort of curls under, like the girls on the vintage posters that Patty has all around her flat. She has brown eyes and drawn-on eyebrows and she wears lots of make-up. I'd rather she didn't wear so much make-up as it hides her natural prettiness, but I do like her red lipstick.

I've masturbated over her in that red lipstick.

And yet I won't masturbate over Dr Hunter.

The virgin and the whore.

There's that pesky self-awareness again.

Another thing about Patty is she has amazing breasts and she's always getting them out. Her nipples are dark pink and they stick out like jelly beans. She knows I like her breasts. This is why she took a photograph of herself with spoons covering her nipples – she was trying to help me make a positive association with spoons. 'Or maybe at least start a spoon fetish going,' she'd told me. Before sticking the picture on my wall I masturbated over it, guiltily and furiously, my fingers covering the spoons, and when I ejaculated, some spurted onto my lip, and that was when I found out that my ejaculate tastes like pistachios, and I haven't eaten pistachios since, so actually her photograph did more harm than good. Because I used to love pistachios.

Anyway. Tonight we go to a café/bar which sells foreign,

expensive beers. There aren't too many people – just a few student-types with cool hair sat around small tables. Patty drinks small glasses of red wine and I drink iced tea from my beaker. Bessie Smith is playing. My mum liked her. She liked lots of old dead female singers. Her absolute favourites were Edith Piaf and Billie Holiday and Mama Cass and Karen Carpenter and Janis Joplin. She used to put on her vinyl records and sing along to her dead females while she did the dishes.

'Do you ever worry about all the shit in the world?' Patty asks me.

'Yes. The world is a bad place,' I say.

'No, I mean shit, all the actual shit. You know – faeces.'

'I try not to think about it.'

She takes a sip of her wine. 'The other day I was sat on the toilet. And I thought, if all the shits I'd ever done were lined up end to end, how long would they be? Like, imagine them lined up around a racetrack. Going round and round like a snail's shell. Would they fill the whole track?'

'Probably.'

'I was sat on the toilet for around twenty minutes this morning trying to work it out in my head. All the variables and stuff.' She takes a licorice Rizla out of her tobacco packet and starts to build a cigarette. 'Taking away a certain number of inches according to age. And considering that shits are gonna be bigger over the Christmas period. Smaller during any teenage bulimia.' She raises her pretend eyebrows wryly, keeping her eyes on the Rizla. 'Anyhoo. The point of the story is there's a scary amount of shit in this world. And I have too much time on my hands.'

She laughs. Patty's laugh is distinctive – a soft, chesty barking. Her bosom jiggles with every bark. Patty's breasts – the non-nipple bits – are large and paper-white with light blue veins, like an aerial view of streams and rivulets seen through cloud.

Rivulets is a lovely word.

'Have you found a job yet?' I say.

She shakes her head. 'There *are* no jobs.' She stands up with the finished cigarette in her fist. 'Back in a sec, Skillacorn,' she says. She always calls me Skillacorn because she thinks it's a good surname and I agree. It has the spiky bits next to the soft bits, like alfacalcidol. She walks out, her stiletto heels tapping against the wooden floor.

She comes back five minutes later looking really sad and smelling strongly of smoke. She sits down, picks up her wine and drinks half of it in one.

'Are you OK, Patty?' I say.

'Yep.' She swallows some more wine, grimacing. 'I just wanna get pissed.'

Patty sometimes gets depressed or angry. But I've never seen her change from happy to sad as sudden as this. Maybe something bad happened when she was having her cigarette. I twist my beaker around in my hand. Twist twist. I put my hands on the table, then in my pockets. I look at the lipstick smears on the empty glasses.

'Let's go find a park like some teenagers,' she says.

'Maybe you shouldn't drink any more, Patty.'

'Maybe I should drink *loads* more.' She takes hold of my arm, even though she knows it makes me uncomfortable, and leads me through the dark streets. She's holding a bottle of red wine she got from a late-night off-licence. I bought Jelly Tots.

There's a small park behind the cycle track. It's locked and surrounded by grisly suffragette spike-railings, but she finds some bent-out bars. She squeezes through the gap, her breasts scraping rust. She drags me to the swings. She sits on one and makes a cigarette. I stand in front of her with my hands in my pockets.

'I feel like I should have a bottle of Woodpecker cider,' she says.

'I feel like I should've stolen some cannabis off my dad,' I say.

'Cannabis,' she says, smiling. She lights her cigarette. 'I like how you say cannabis instead of weed or ganja or whatever.'

'It's a good word. Canna-bisss.'

'I never thought of it like that.' She drinks from her wine bottle. Some dribbles down her chin. She doesn't wipe it away. 'I never thought about the actual ... wordiness of the word.'

'I like words,' I say.

'You should be a poet,' she says.

'My poems would just be lists of words I like.'

'Who's to say that doesn't constitute poetry?'

I shrug. She flicks ash and crosses one leg over the other. She's wearing a short dress. Her legs are bare and so pale they kind of glow in the dark. 'So, do you have any canna-bisss?'

'I don't take drugs. I've told you a million times.'

'Oh, right. Yeah.' She smiles. Looks at me. She looks at me like she's thinking of something. She looks at me a long time. I don't like it. She drinks her wine and smokes her brown cigarette. Gazes up at the sky. 'Look at the moon,' she says.

It's blue-white, like her legs, and almost whole. The sky is navy blue and the stars are silvery bright. I wonder if the moon had anything to do with Patty's mood change earlier. I know that happens with some women.

'I like the moon,' she says.

'Patty? Why did you get so sad earlier?'

She doesn't say anything. I move my legs to stop them going stiff. She swings back and forth a while, trailing her heels through the woodchips. She comes to a stop. 'Tell me a story, Skillacorn. Something with sex in it.'

'No.' I often tell Patty stories and lots of them have sex in, but tonight I feel uncomfortable about it.

'Go on. It'll make me feel better.' She puts her hands together and mouths 'please'.

'All right then. OK. Let's see. So, there was a boy with white-blond hair and apple-green eyes, and one day he went to the doctors to get some diclofenac, which is an anti-inflammatory analgesic, and the doctor he went to see was a beautiful woman with Japanese hair, and when he was called in to see her, he found that she was naked, and he thought that this was very strange.'

'Understandably,' says Patty.

'Yes. But he went in and he sat on the chair by her desk, and he was very embarrassed but he pretended not to notice, and the doctor, she was just sat there with her breasts out, and they were lovely breasts, like yours, Patty, except with paler nipples, and he couldn't see her vagina, but he could smell it – ' Patty laughs – 'not because it was a strong-smelling vagina, but because he had a supernaturally powerful sense of smell, which he'd acquired by magic, but that's a whole other story.'

'Tell it,' says Patty.

'I thought you wanted a story with sex in it?'

'Make it sexy then.'

I breathe out a sigh. 'OK. So, he acquired the sense of smell by magic. By a witch, an evil, sexy witch. See, she'd seen this boy out and about and she'd fancied him with a savage lust. And she'd followed him one day back to his flat, and she was in the form of a cat, a black cat—'

'Original,' says Patty.

'OK, a tortoiseshell cat, with a limp and a crooked tail and one eye green and one eye red. And a bald patch in the shape of Australia in her fur.'

Patty smiles.

'And anyway, when this boy went into his flat, the witch followed, going through his legs, only he didn't notice, her being a cat, but as soon as the door was closed, she turned back into a woman, a naked woman. And she had a beautiful body with large breasts, only they were a bit droopy because she'd had a lot of children, but the boy didn't mind, he wasn't fussy, and he got a huge erection, huge, which was strange because normally his penis was just average, but the thing about this witch is she had this magic charm which made all the men she was about to have sex with grow big penises, temporarily anyway, and the witch had done this charm herself, because she liked big penises—'

'Size queen,' says Patty.

'Yes. Anyway. They had sex in the hallway, and it was good satisfying sex, only it didn't last long because they were both so aroused.'

'Describe the sex.'

I shuffle my feet in the woodchips. 'Um, OK. So the boy took off all his clothes first, and the witch just stood there watching with this dry smile on her face, which the boy found disconcerting, but he carried on anyway, and soon he was completely naked with his enormous erection, and another thing – the size of his penis was now exactly six inches long and—'

'That's not enormous,' says Patty.

'I know. But here's the thing – it was three inches *thick*, because this was the witch's preference. See, she liked her penises thick more than long to accommodate her vagina, which was big after all the children she'd had. Do you want to know how many children she'd had?'

Patty nods.

'Two thousand, one hundred and eighty-five.'

'Yowza,' says Patty.

'Yes,' I say.

'Describe the sex,' she says.

'OK. So then they were both naked—'

'Hang on,' says Patty. 'If the witch could make men's dicks fatter with her magic, how come she didn't just make her pussy tighter?'

'She was a feminist, like you,' I say. 'She didn't believe that she should have to obey the beauty myth.'

'Touché, Skillacorn. How many children was it?'

'Two thousand, one hundred and eighty-five.'

'Well done.' She waves her hand. 'Now describe the sex. In detail. Tell me about his fat cock sliding into her baggy cunt.'

51

I feel my cheeks get hot. 'OK. Um. So they're both naked, and his penis is sticking out, and she's wet. And he's, um, he's…' I shake my head. 'I can't do this, Patty. It's pornography.'

She smiles, her stiletto heels digging into the woodchip. 'Come here.'

'Pardon?'

'Come here.'

'OK.' I take a step closer.

'Come *here*,' she says.

My heart starts beating hard. I take another dumb step. Now my knees are touching hers. She reaches up, grabs my shirt collar and drags me down. She kisses me on the lips. She holds on to the back of my neck and sticks her tongue in my mouth. I can taste cigarettes and metallic spit and licorice. She sucks on my lower lip and makes her tongue touch my tongue. I try to kiss back. My tongue feels like a stupid lump of meat. I'm not doing it right. I can taste the perfumed waxiness of her red lipstick, I can feel it smearing my lips. I should be erect. But I'm just scared. Because I'm not doing it right.

We end up on the splintery floor. Maybe she's too drunk to realise how bad I am. Woodchip digs into my back. I can feel the bulge of my Jelly Tots in the back pocket of my jeans. She's on top of me. My thoughts are zipping around my head like charged electrons. I'm not doing it right. I won't be able to do it right. I'm scared, I'm flaccid. Zip zip zip.

I think, get it together.

She sucks on my lip. Grinds into me.

I think, come on, Skillacorn. *Come on.*

She moves down my body. I just lay there like road kill. And then I hear a lumpy retching and feel a soft spatter of something warm and wet hit my belly. I rise up on my elbows. Patty is vomiting into the woodchip next to my hip. Frothy dark vomit. Bits of it splashing my skin and shirt.

She rolls off and sits there all slumped, her chin slimy. The blue-white moon is up there, high and bright and horribly omniscient.

The first taxi refuses to take her. The second man nods when she gets in and takes my money. I give him Patty's address and shut the door. I watch the car drive away into tree-lined darkness.

I walk home with my hands in my pockets. The air is cold against my sick-damp shirt. The streets are empty, which is scary sometimes, all the dark cars stretched out end to end, the occasional street light, the sleeping houses. The imagination can run wild. The cars can be filled with things, all sorts of things. But tonight, the emptiness is good, I welcome it.

I see a man walking toward me. He's middle-aged but he's got a walking stick which he trails along at his side. Like he doesn't need it. He gets closer. His eyes are fixed straight ahead into the middle distance. As he reaches me I get this feeling that he's suddenly going to lash his stick at my head. Not just a feeling – a certainty. My heart goes like a dropped elevator.

He passes by.

The same thing happens with the next man who passes – I imagine his fist flying out of the dark like a cobra, and my mind and body seize up with panic. I'm certain. Convinced. Like Patty with her spear bones. He's going to kill me. Kill me kill me kill me. But, of course, he passes by.

The rest of the way I cross the road when I see someone. I walk fast, looking back over my shoulder all the time. My heart beats like crazy. I go over the different ways of saying didanosine.

Didano-seen.

Dee-*dan*-o-seen.

Di-*dan*-o-seen.

Di-*day*-no-seen.

Dee-*day*-no-seen.

Dee-*day*-no-sign.

Dih-*dan*-o-sign.

And on and on.

Next I go through phendimetrazine. Then gadodiamide. When I reach the Hog and Duck, I'm saying timolol, timolol, timolol, over and over again. Timolol is a beta blocker my great-nan used to take. It's also used as an eye drop for glaucoma, which she also had, in her one eye, just the one. There aren't lots of different ways of saying timolol. I just like the word. Tim-o-lol. The soft 'lol' at the end. It relaxes me like a Buddhist chant.

I see a group of teenage boys coming out of a chip shop and it's too late to cross the road. My heart starts up again. I walk past, shoulders like clenched fists. The boys are eating sausages in batter. I can smell vinegar. Timolol. Timolol. Vinegar vinegar. Vinegol, vinegol. Timololll. They ignore me. I'm safe. Timolol. My heart keeps going and my arms feel numb. I'm getting overanxious. Careful, Sylvester, careful, I think. Distraction, Sylvester, distraction. 'Timolol, Sylvester, timolol,' I whisper.

So. There was this boy called Sylvester Skillacorn and he had white-blond hair and green eyes which sparkled like polished emeralds or apples, whichever you like best, and one night he was passing this lane when a woman grabbed him by the arm and pulled him in, whispering, 'Come, Sylvester, come with me.' Of course, Sylvester couldn't see her face because she had a black scarf covering her head and hanging over her eyes. The lane was chilly and it smelled like metal and stones and dust and it was silent, it was so silent that the silence was loud, like an invisible train rushing toward them, and then there was this huge dead rat the size of a cat lying on its side in the middle of the lane and there were other, smaller rats feasting on its guts, and one of them nipped at his ankles, so he kicked at it and it flew through the air and hit the wall and exploded into a hundred tinier rats. And Sylvester, he could now smell grease and sick and wine in the air. And licorice, he could smell licorice, of course he could, and he noticed all the multiplying rat babies were wearing red lipstick – no, that's silly, they weren't wearing red lipstick, and anyway, the

54

woman reached the end of the lane and it was a dead end. And she crouched down in front of the tall brick wall and placed her hand against it and said, 'Naproxen, naproxen, die-clo*fen*ac!' just like that, the f like an f, no funny business, and there was a roaring and a rumbling and a chunk of wall turned to dust and the dust flew away and the woman crawled through the gap and signalled Sylvester to follow and there was a tunnel, a long, long tunnel, and he crawled behind her, his nose an inch from her backside, which smelled like musk and warmth. And licorice, it smelled like licorice, can't forget the licorice. Anyway, they crawled for a long, long time, and the woman kept saying, 'Not long now, not long now,' and Sylvester wondered why he was following at all, he should be at home, masturbating over his wicked stepmother, The Sultry Duchess of Ely, well, not *literally* over her, that would be very inappropriate, and anyway, eventually they came to the end and emerged into a forest, a beautiful lushly green forest with rubbery leaved plants and giant coconut trees and bright blue flowers and lots of bird song and monkey squawks, and the woman told Sylvester that they had arrived in the secret kingdom of Timolol. Then she lifted the scarf off her head and her face was a rotting corpse face with fat maggots dribbling out of her crusty mouth hole – no, that's horrible, Sylvester, that's not what happened. She was a beautiful woman, Sylvester, with Japanese hair and red lipstick. Oh, thank God, thank God…

The lights are on but Dad's in bed, so I guess he remembered this time. I go to my room, swallow a diclofenac (die-*clov*-enac), take off my dirty shirt and sit on the bed.

I eat my Jelly Tots one at a time, slowly, by colour.

The Virgin and the Whore

At the end of my street I see a dead seagull lying on its back. An omen, I think. I should have stayed in bed. I should still be there, staring at the ceiling and feeling sorry for myself with my broken penis and my dead mother. Worrying about Patty – she must feel even worse than me, assuming she remembers anything. But I came out for a walk and an expensive bowel movement and now there's a dead seagull as well as a dead mother.

Stupid, stupid, stupid.

When I get home, Dad and Delyth are getting ready to leave. Dad picks his car keys out of the fruit bowl on his coffee table and Delyth gives me an insincere but well-meant smile.

'"Glad you could drop in,"' says Dad in his Stallone voice. He shakes his keys in the air. '"Do you like jewellery?"'

'"Oh fuck you,"' I say, and even though it's OK for me to use bad language when it's from a quote I still get a shiver up my spine.

Dad's mouth drags down at the edges. '"I prefer blondes."'

Delyth smacks him on the arm. 'Oi! Natural brunette standing right here!'

'It's from *Tango and Cash*,' says Dad. 'Ever seen it?'

'No.'

Dad shakes his head, clucking with pretend disappointment. 'No culture.'

'What are you like?' she says, pressing her breasts against his arm.

'Going to Asda,' says Dad to me. 'Coming?'

I shake my head. I don't want to be in a car today. Not with the omens going the way they are.

I should probably talk about the blinking. It started about the same time as the touching and the scraping. I was on a school trip to Bristol Zoo. That morning my mum had stuck plasters on the ends of my first two fingers and thumbs. I'd peeled them off as soon as I got on the coach, but now I was left with tacky glue on my fingertips, and it wouldn't come off. On the back of the seat in front of me there was a black plastic ashtray, the kind that opens up on hinges like an oyster and shuts with a snap. I reached out to touch it and my sticky finger sort of bumped across the surface. If I couldn't do my patterns then maybe a Bad Thing would happen, like maybe we'd crash and all die with our skulls crushed in and bits of glass spiking through our guts, or, at the zoo, a gorilla would grab through the bars and break Miss Fletcher's neck and she'd die with her eyes like perfect circles.

I stared out of the window. It was raining. The trees and asphalt went past in a watery blur. I started focusing on the cars driving beside us. I started to blink every time we passed one. A quick fluttery blink for a car going fast, a long, scrunchy-eyed blink for a slow one. Blnk, blnk, bliiiink. Corresponding with the length, like an eyelid Morse code. And it *was* a code. A pattern. Bliiiiiiink, blnk, blnk, blnk.

Miss Fletcher tried to talk to me. 'Are you OK, Sylvester?'

I kept my eyes on the window. Blnk, blnk, blnk. 'Yes, Miss.'

'Are you – are you sure? Do you want a Rolo?'

'No, thank you, Miss.'

'Why don't you look at me when you're talking, Sylvester?'

'I don't want to.'

Miss Fletcher sat next to me that whole journey. Sometimes she tried to speak to me, the rest of the time she just watched as I blinked my blinks. I couldn't see her looking, but I felt her eyes like healing hands on the side of my head. Miss Fletcher knew all about me. I was the blond boy who once spent a whole afternoon tracing his finger around the light switch in the Naughty Corner of the classroom while the other children played with sand and water.

I was the boy who couldn't have spoons.

It wasn't so bad with the blinking though. I mean, it was the same sensation – the feeling of being locked in, unable to stop before the right time, the wordless worry of a bee pulling its stinger out, fearing disembowelment. But all car journeys come to an end. I have no power over that and so I can't be held accountable. I can't do it outside the car. It only works *inside*. That's the rule. That's the magic. Car stops, engine cools, no more blinks. Light switches don't disappear. Spoons don't turn to dust in your hands and drift away on the breeze.

I won't do it anymore. I sit in the front, low down in my seat so I can't see the tarmac ahead, and look straight ahead, never out the side. I've trained my neck to be still. Strict trapezii like Greek columns. I make words out of the number plates on the backs of cars, which is distraction and good exercise for the brain and has nothing to do with magic, or so I tell myself. If there are no cars ahead, I make pictures from the clouds, from birds, words from crumbs on the dashboard.

You can make a cloud look like anything. Crumbs say anything.

Like, 'Sylvester Skillacorn Is OK And One Day He Will Fall In Love'.

I stand outside the house drinking probiotic water and feeling the night air cool my sweaty skin. TV light flashes through the gap between the living room curtains. I go in and do some stretches in the hallway, which is a very important thing to do after running or you can end up with bad knees. I feel better after the exercise, especially after noticing that the dead seagull I'd seen this morning has been taken away. An omen reversed. TV sounds rumble through the living room door. Bombs exploding, machine gun fire. An action film. *Commando*, probably. I squeeze open the door. The room is dark, Dad's large plasma screen lighting it up sporadically like lightning. I walk toward the door at the other side, treading softly. There's an explosion in the film and the room lights up.

My father is performing cunnilingus on Delyth.

More explosions.

Delyth is sat on the couch with her legs spread. Eyes closed. Skirt hitched up to her belly. Dad is on his knees on the floor, face buried between her large thighs. His head is moving, slowly nodding. Like an old dog eating its dinner. The TV explosions stop and the room darkens, but I can still see them, grainy and shadowy. There are bottles of wine silhouetted on the table. I get going, feet landing ninja-silent on the carpet. The film changes scene. Daylight. Room lights up. I'm passing the coffee table. I look at Delyth. And her eyes are open. Big black eyes. Looking at me. My heart twitches. Her lips curve into a smile. She grabs my dad's silver hair and groans. 'Mmm, mmm.'

I get out, fast.

Inside my room I walk around in nervous circles. My erection is a baseball bat.

I climb into bed and take care of it, my face stuffed into the pillow.

The next morning I masturbate three times. Kate Bush's slippery, scarlet mouth keeps getting nudged out of my mind by Delyth's nasty smile as she grinds into my father's face.

It's OK. My father isn't included. Just a grey presence on the periphery. A smudgy thumb on the edge of a quickly taken photograph.

It's OK. We're all perverted. Bust open the average person's subconscious and it's like sewer water gushing out.

Nothing wrong with Sylvester Skillacorn. Besides the obvious.

I rush out of the house some time after noon. The sky isn't so lovely today. Grey-tinged clouds block out the sun. As I walk down the garden path I see Aled Mellor. He's got a lawnmower overturned on the patio and he's scraping out old mossy grass packed between the blades. With a spoon. Bad sign. As I open the front gate, he whips his head around and frowns at me. Like I'm a bad teenager.

When I was fifteen I had my first and only girlfriend. Her name was Jenny. Her mum was a really fat woman with diabetes who had to use a walking stick and her dad was dead. Carbon monoxide poisoning. My mum had died a year before, so I felt an affinity, like we both belonged in the Dead Parent Club. Jenny was pretty and nice, though everyone in school picked on her because she once leaked menstrual blood onto the back of her school skirt and walked around with it until last break. The menstrual stain had been shaped like a teddy bear's head, at least that's what everyone said, and so they called her Reddy Teddy for years and years. I liked her. She was kind to animals and she had a crush on Rowan Atkinson in his beard years. She hated modern chart music and only listened to The Carpenters and The Mamas and Papas and Abba. On vinyl. She had blue eyes that were so pale the iris looked almost white in the middle, the rim porcelain-blue. Like little toilets. She fancied me, even though I had to see the school counsellor every day and I was shorter than most boys my age.

It lasted two months.

She'd initiated sex one night while her mum was out at a Weight Watchers meeting. She did all these things, like kissing up and down my body and putting her tongue in my belly button, and I had the feeling she'd got it all out of a magazine, 'Top Tips to Turn On Your Man' or something, and she must have taken my terrified whimpers for moans of arousal because

61

she took my trousers and boxer shorts off and pulled me on top of her. Then there was twenty minutes of trying to stuff my semi-flaccid penis inside her. I couldn't help it. I was petrified – close to vomiting from fear. I'd barely got used to kissing by this point. Holding hands even felt too much.

Afterwards, she lay there with ceramic eyes focused on the ceiling while Mama Cass sang 'Make Your Own Kind of Music' on the old Decca.

I pretended it was a good idea when she broke up with me, like I agreed with her. Like I'd been contemplating it myself. After a few months she started going out with Paul Banks from the sixth form, who had a tongue piercing and sang in a metal band called Autopsy Bastard. She probably had lots of good sex with him. I would imagine them doing it, all sweaty and grunting, and it would make me feel sick with sadness. Poor lonely Sylvester with his dough-soft penis, poor, poor Sylvester, who watches Jenny and Paul kissing and thigh-stroking in the canteen and walks home to his motherless house and slopes up to his bedroom and masturbates under the covers because the ghosts of his dead relatives might be watching.

Later that day. My inner mind understood that I'd end up on this bench – it just took a while for my feet to catch up. I eat one of my Jazz apples while I watch the houses. No one's gone in or out yet. The clouds have darkened. The air feels loaded.

I shouldn't be here.

Hunting Dr Hunter.

At half-past two it starts raining. Hard. I take my apples and head home. The once pale-grey pavement is now slate-grey.

And then. Dr Hunter, holding a transparent umbrella. Blue leggings, white and black stripy top. She doesn't look like a doctor. She looks like a beautiful woman from a Specsavers advert. Her Japanese hair is dry and perfect. I want to smell it. I stare at her. Standing in the rain, hair stuck to my forehead, an apple in each hand. Big green eyes blasting out terrified love. Green eyes green apples green eyes green apples.

'Hello.'

'Oh, hello, Sylvester,' she says.

Not hesitating over my name even though she must have thousands of patients.

'An apple a day keeps the doctor away,' she says.

I smile, dumbly. A raindrop drips off the end of my nose. I hold out one of the apples. 'Would you like one?'

She looks at the apple, her mouth slightly open. She doesn't want the apple.

'They're nice,' I say. 'Jazz apples. They're my favourite. Except, if you have one a day, you'll keep yourself away.' I glance down at the ground. 'Which makes no sense.'

'Jazz apples? Well.' She laughs a little. 'Uh. OK. Thank you.' She takes one. Her cold finger skims my own. 'Take care.' She waves the apple. 'Thank you.'

She crosses the road with her leggings showing every delicious wobble and heads toward the cluster of houses I've twice staked out. Stalked out. She gets her key out. Opens the gate to one-seventeen.

I start walking.

One-seventeen, one-seventeen, one-seventeeeeen…

Part of me is excited because she stopped and talked to me when she shouldn't have stopped and talked to me. And part of me is embarrassed because I gave her an apple and I know she didn't want the apple.

Letting Out the Bull

Dad is in the kitchen glaring out of the window. He sees me, my wet hair and soaked clothes. 'Fucking Mellor's been in and out of his house like a blue-arsed fly,' he says. 'Watching the house from his conservatory. Fucking spying.'

I open the fridge and take out a carton of juice.

'Tiny-minded prick. That's what he is.' He makes his hand into a claw and brings it to his chest, doing a face. 'With his tiny fucking Jeremy Beadle hand.' He shakes his head with disgust.

'I think he's suspicious,' I say. 'The drugs.'

Dad looks at me. 'Don't start with the paranoia, Sylv, not today.'

'What's wrong with today?'

'I'm just not in the mood.' He places his hands on the kitchen counter and leans on it. He's wearing jogging bottoms and a white T-shirt. No shoes or socks. His feet are exactly like mine – skinny and white and hairless, except he has a small toe missing on the left foot from an accident he had when he worked at the steelworks. 'I won't lie,' he says, looking down at a bowl of used teabags in front of him, 'I do get paranoid sometimes. But I try very hard not to indulge it.' He looks at me. 'Never indulge it.'

I drink my juice.

'I do this thing sometimes,' he says, poking the used teabags in a mindless way. 'When I get weed paranoia, I do this thing. I get all these ... all these frightening thoughts. End of the world, dying, dementia, that kind of thing. Tsunamis, atomic bombs. You know. I'll be sitting there, usually in front of the TV, and if nothing else works – you know, music, films, that kind of thing – if nothing else *distracts*, I imagine all the bad thoughts in my head as monsters. Slimy monsters. Like bacteria. Invading my mind.'

He glances at me. 'Why am I telling you this?'

'It's interesting,' I say.

He smiles. Turns his attention back to the teabags. 'I thought *you'd* find this interesting.' He shakes his head. 'I imagine the bad thoughts are bacteria monsters attacking my brain. And then I imagine my defences. Like soldiers. Small soldiers. I imagine their uniforms, their faces. Even their back stories. Their wives waiting back home, all that stuff. I imagine them fighting the bacteria monsters – shit, this sounds crazy.' He shakes his head again, still smiling. 'But it works. It really does. I imagine the kind of attacks they'd use on the monsters. Ripping into their bodies with bayonets, exploding them with bombs, that kind of thing. Tactical stuff. I go into real detail. I even imagine the rousing speech the general makes to inspire his soldiers. Like that bit in *Lord of the Rings*? With King Theoden? Fucking ridiculous… Anyway. The reason it works is because by the time I've finished imagining all this I've forgotten what the paranoid thoughts were in the first place.'

He brings his hands together with a massive clap and looks at me again. 'There you go, Sylvester. An insight into your dear old dad.'

'I'm glad you told me.'

Dad sighs and stands up straight. He flicks on the kettle and takes a mug – his favourite Cardiff Blues mug – from the mug tree.

'Your mum's anniversary's coming up,' he says. I can't see his face because he's got his back to me again.

I nod. 'Four years.'

'You coming this time?'

I shrug but of course he can't see me, so I add, 'Not sure.'

'No pressure,' he says, quickly.

I haven't visited Mum's grave since she died. Dad goes three times a year: her birthday, the anniversary of her death and Christmas. He takes a bottle of good red wine, a spliff and an MP3 player and gets drunk by her headstone, listening to a playlist of Mum's long-dead females. He always comes home maudlin and drinks himself into a quiet stupor on the couch, except on Christmas Day when he's expected to jolly himself around for the various friends/customers and relatives who come visiting. Dad doesn't usually ask me if I'm coming or not because it's a subject strewn with eggshells. Guilt on my part probably. Because I *should* visit my mother's grave, even if it's just once. This time though he's got an ulterior motive: he's reminding me that *he's* going. He's letting me know that he's never going to stop going, even with a new woman in his life. That he will hold my mum's memory sacred.

Or maybe I'm reading too much into it.

'Where's Delyth?' I ask.

'At her mother's. Having Sunday dinner.'

Dad makes tea. When he's finished he glances once more out of the kitchen window and then closes the curtain with a snap. 'Wanna watch a film?' he says.

'Um. OK. Yeah.'

'"Tell me something, Conan: what is best in life?"'

I smile. '"To crush your enemies, see them driven before you and to hear da lamentations of da women."' I make my voice go as low as possible for this last bit and it comes out pretty accurate.

He swigs his tea. 'Very good. Shall I make a bowl of popcorn?'

I look at him.

'Only joking.' He walks past me and ruffles my hair.

Arnold Schwarzenegger is Dad's second favourite action movie star (and my first). *Total Recall* is his favourite Arnold film but he's watched it too many times and ruined it for himself, like I've done listening to Radiohead's third album and eating mashed sweet potato. So it's *Red Heat* tonight. We're on the sofa. A cushion between us. Dad drinks tea and smokes cigarettes and sucks on Vera, holding big lungfuls of vapour in, with a face all constipated. At six points during the film he has to stop and pause the film so he can deal with customers. He makes them hang around in the hallway while he gets their orders – quarters, half-quarters, ten bags, ounces. Blocks of dark brown hash wrapped in tight, perfect cling film. He tells them they can't come in because he's watching a film with his family. And it's weird hearing that and remembering that me and Dad are 'family'. 'I'm entitled to some family time, you know,' he tells them. Some days he doesn't like people sitting all over his floor eating his biscuits and spilling squiggles of tobacco on his carpet.

Delyth comes home.

'How are my boys?' she says, spilling through the door.

Dad pauses the DVD. 'We're watching a film, Del.'

Delyth brings a finger to her lips and shushes herself. She comes over and sits on the couch between me and Dad. Her buttocks take up the whole cushion. She smells of alcohol and cigarettes. She leans forward and picks up Vera.

'Careful with that,' says Dad.

'I'm not a fucking baby,' she says.

'You're pissed as a fart, Del.'

'Indeed I am, Carl. Indeed I am.'

She presses her lips to the mouthpiece and sucks up vapour. Holds it in. Breathes it out. 'What's that saying?' she says. 'Beer before grass, you're in the – how does it go?'

Dad slowly lights a cigarette and looks at her. 'Beer before grass, you're on your arse; grass before beer, you're in the clear.'

'Well, I haven't had beer, have I? I've had wine.'

Dad's eyes crinkle, cigarette dangling from his curved lips, smoke curling. He loves her. 'You try and shut up for ten minutes,' he says. 'We're gonna watch the end of this film.'

She looks at him with mock innocence and presses her finger to her lips. Dad leans back and presses play. She puts her hand on Dad's knee. Squeezes it playfully. He takes her hand, curls his fingers through hers. Her thigh presses against my thigh. Warm contractions. Soft flesh. I can't follow the film anymore. I'm thinking about last night. Wondering if she remembers it.

Wondering what she tastes like.

I stand up and leave the room. No excuses, no good nights. I go to my bedroom and sit on the edge of the bed. I will not masturbate. He loves her. I will not masturbate. I think about horrible things. Dead things. Faces rotting in graves, maggots squirming through the nose holes, nipples all tripe-grey and covered in beetles. I get on the floor and do twenty-five Spiderman push-ups followed by fifty sit-ups followed by fifty leg raises. It's not enough. I do fifty squats, another twenty-five Spiderman push-ups. I go to the bathroom, have a shower, brush my teeth for two minutes. I come back to my room, wet, a red towel – red signifying nothing – wrapped around my hips. I close my curtains. There's a knock at my door.

'Yes?'

The door opens. Delyth. 'Mind if I come in a sec?' she says.

I just stand there, droplets of shower water shrinking on my body.

She comes in. 'Thought I'd pop in for a chat while your dad makes me coffee.' She looks at my bald chest as she speaks. 'He wants to sober me up, dunee?'

She sits on my bed, pats a space next to her. 'Come and sit by yer a minute, chick.'

I silently obey.

'What made you run off so quick? Eh? One minute you're sitting there all nice, watching a film with us, the next minute you're running away like your arse is on fire.' She places a hand on my wet shoulder. Her head bobs slightly with the drink. 'What's that about?'

'I don't know,' I say. 'I just – I've seen that film so many times.'

She looks at me dubiously. Her hand slips down my bicep, rests on my wrists. 'I want us to be friends, Sylvester.'

'OK.'

'You and me, we both love your father. We got that in common, yeah?'

I look down at my hands. 'Sure. Yes.'

'I know you've got some weird mental stuff going on, Sylvester, and I don't give a shit. OK? Origh'?'

I nod.

'You be yourself around me, babe. We're family now.'

She stands up, opens her arms. 'Come yer.'

I stand up, slowly. She wraps her arms around me. Presses her body against mine. Crotch to crotch. Large soft breasts squished against my chest. Her vulnerable bits against my vulnerable bits. I get an erection again.

Some kind of family.

I pull away, smiling unconvincingly.

'What the fuck is going on here?'

Dad is standing at the doorway, holding a cup of coffee. He stares at us with his mouth open and then he throws the mug at the wall. It explodes and milky coffee splashes all over the wallpaper, the plug socket. Delyth screams, her hands flying up to her face.

Dad strides up to me, mouth a slit. 'What the *fuck* are you doing with a boner?' He grabs my throat with one hand and pushes me until I'm up against the wall. He squeezes and stares into my eyes. 'What's wrong with this picture, Sylvester?' The words are an angry whisper. I struggle, try and prise his strong fingers away. My towel falls off. 'You want to fuck my girlfriend, do you?' I shake my head, eyes popping. Delyth is screaming.

He gives my throat one final squeeze and lets go. I gasp in some air. Cover myself with my hands. Dad is still staring at me. His eyes are wet, his face pink. He punches the wall next to my head.

Bits of powdery plaster trickle down the wall, landing on my shoulder. Dad turns and walks out of the room. He doesn't even look at Delyth. She's crying, one hand covering her mouth. She follows him out, saying, 'Carl, babe, don't be like that. *Carl.*' I stand there cupping myself, my back pressed against the cold wall. Dad reappears in the doorway. Keeping his eyes on mine he reaches for the light switch – his knuckles are ragged and bloody – and turns out the light.

The Man Who Forsook Coasters

Dad is going to come back in and beat me up.

Dad is going to kick me out of the flat.

Delyth is going to tell Dad about last night and she'll exaggerate it and make out I stood there watching her receive cunnilingus like a big pervert instead of passing through the living room as fast as possible, and Dad is going to come in here and punch my face into a bloody, pulpy non-face.

Delyth is going to tell lies to make herself look like a better person and Dad is going to come back in and break my legs the way he broke Gary the Goth's leg for hitting on Mum in the cloakroom of Pinky's Bar and Grill fifteen years ago.

Dad is going to break my nose again.

I'm going to be homeless.

I'll end up in a hostel surrounded by men even more frightening than my father.

These are just my surface fears. And as well as the fears there's shame, squirming shame. I keep seeing myself being throttled against the wall. Through Delyth's eyes. Wriggling, struggling, naked. Shrinking penis flapping about like a dead earthworm shaken by a toddler, red gasping face, bulging eyes. Ugly, ugly, ugly. I sit in the dark, palm on my heart. My body's starting to feel numb, like my blood has gone ice-cold. I stand up and grope in the dark until I find my bed. I take my pyjama bottoms from under my pillow and put them on. I open my curtains and climb out of the window into the back garden. I lie on the wet grass and close my eyes. Breathe deep and slow. 'Timolol,' I say to the warm black night. 'Timolol.'

There was a boy and he had white-blond hair and eyes that sparkled like emeralds, and he – he lived in this little house in a small village called Timolol and there were fourteen dead men buried in his garden, and they all had beautiful faces, or at least they once did, but now they're rotting and full of worms, and anyway, they're buried in this boy's garden, except the boy didn't kill them, the wicked witch did, but that's a whole other story, and this boy, he goes out into his back garden every morning and he prays for the souls of the fourteen dead men, each one, individually, and he spends three minutes on each prayer, exactly three minutes, not one second more or less, and he follows the time with a beautiful stopwatch, which he stole from a minotaur in a labyrinth, but that's a whole other story. So the dead men. Well, what can I say about the dead men? They were once warriors, amazing warriors, and the thing that had made them special was their vision. They could see better than normal people, because they had been blessed by the good witch of Alfacalcidol, who had long flowing Japanese hair though she wasn't Japanese, and anyway, she had blessed them one frosty morning on the top of a high mountain, and she'd used her special powers, and the next morning they all woke up with superhuman hawk vision. And they went on to do all sorts of heroic things and win battles – but good battles, not bad battles like the ones we have today, and they always won, because of their vision, and also their bravery and strength, they had lots of that too, but not because of a blessing, they were just born that way. And...
Anyway. They were such heroes that the wicked witch of Timolol hunted them down one by one and plucked out their eyes and ate them and had sex with them and then murdered them in horrible ways. And how they ended up buried in the boy's garden, well, that's a whole other story.

74

I rub my temples and look up at the stars.

Sometimes I wonder if I should just accept all the mind-calming drugs the doctors have been offering all these years. Because I cannot escape my own brain. And I get so tired.

And Valium is such a beautiful word.

My back has got cold from the wet grass so I go back inside. I don't dare go to the bathroom. I urinate into an old Dr. Martens shoe. I place it on the windowsill and some sloshes on my hand. I clean it off with an antibacterial wipe. I try not to think about the bacteria in my teeth. I chew some peppermint gum. I take off my damp pyjama bottoms and get into bed. I can't hear anything next door. Maybe they've made up, Dad and Delyth, and now they're cuddling in bed together, laughing about teenage boys with their silly erections.

Delyth saying, 'Boys will be boys, Carl,' and Dad saying, 'But you don't want a boy, do you? You want a man.'

Dad and Delyth laughing and then kissing sloppily, her slowly moving a hand toward his horse-sized penis.

Delyth coming in here and sliding her wet vagina up my bare thigh, my dad standing over us, masturbating angrily then spraying his ejaculate over us like champagne.

I roll over and shout, 'Fucking fuck!' into the pillow.

It's the first time I've used bad language without quotation marks in over ten years.

Three days I stay in my room. Listening to my father through the walls. Opening and closing doors and thudding around like a minotaur in his labyrinth.

I don't hear Delyth.

I use the Dr. Martens to urinate into, emptying it out the window after each use. I still have the carrier bag of food I bought from Pulse 'n' Grain a few days ago. Hanging from my wardrobe door like an old testicle. Seeds and nuts and a couple of flapjacks and the big bag of plantain or cassava crisps or whatever they are. But I don't have an appetite anyway.

Just after midnight I need to empty my bowels. I can hear Dad still awake in the living room. I climb out into the garden. The kitchen light is off. I creep through the dark grass to the hydrangea bushes at the end of the lawn. I look up at the windows upstairs – the students' flat. Dark windows. I squat in the dark and go to the toilet. A round cluster of purplish-blue flowers stares at me like a curious alien. I look at the steaming bowel movement afterwards and it's huge. The hydrangea seems to wilt its head in disgust. I climb back into my bedroom. I clean myself with antibacterial wipes and hide them in my bin.

An hour later I hear Dad going into his bedroom. I wait half an hour until I'm sure he's in bed. I sneak out of my room and go to the kitchen. I grab a carton of orange juice and a large bottle of mineral water from the fridge and my special beaker and a packet of Hobnobs and a bunch of brown-speckled bananas from my shelf in the larder. The recycling bin is bulging with empty cans of Guinness. I go to the bathroom for my toothbrush and toothpaste. I look in the living room. There are empty Guinness cans on the carpet. The air is muggy with old smoke. There's a filthy ashtray on the coffee table. Without a coaster.

The next day I read books in bed and do exercises and stretches on my carpet. No bowel movement on this day. I continue to splash shoe-fulls of urine out of the window. The warm sun evaporates all the water out of it, concentrates it to pure ammonia, and outside smells like a London subway.

In the afternoon I hear Delyth's voice. I hear her crying and Dad shouting. The front door slamming. Then silence.

In the evening I think about leaving. Going to an empty pub to read and drink lemonade. The cinema, a café. But the thought of ghosting through the streets makes my skin feel all prickly. I'd get extra anxious outside, the mood I'm in. I stay on the bed, tortoise-chewing my dry snacks, listening out for my father's slow tombstone tread. The house is busy tonight. I can hear his customers/friends talking and laughing. Using the toilet, going to the kitchen to make tea. Dad's Scott Walker album plays loudly from the living room. Aled Mellor is probably grinding his dentures together in a bitter filth next door.

By two in the morning all the voices have gone. I can hear Tom Waits now – 'I Hope I Don't Fall In Love With You'. Dad stays in the living room until the album is finished and then he goes to bed. I sneak to the kitchen for supplies. There are more empty cans than ever, Stella Artois this time. Toast crumbs and onion skin and buttery knives mess up the counter. The living room is just as untidy, but the coffee table is clear. As it should be. There's a photo of Mum propped up against the fruit bowl. A Polaroid of her sat on the beach in her turquoise and white bikini. She's smiling awkwardly, like a shy teenager, though she must have been twenty-something at the time. Her long white-blonde hair is wet and stringy. She has a half-smoked cigarette held between her fingers. Her nails are painted pink. At the edge of the shot is a tiny white hand gripping a red plastic spade.

I leave the photo where it is and go back to bed. I think about Dad. Him sitting on the couch, elbows on knees, staring down at the Polaroid of his dead wife. Crying. He would have been crying.

I have this one really vivid memory of my dad from when I was little. It's what I try to recall when I have trouble thinking kindly of him. He'd taken me blackberry picking, which you can take as symbolic if you want, like in the Seamus Heaney poem I learnt at school where blackberry picking is all about sex, but actually it was a very straightforward thing – it was blackberry season and Mum had lots of leftover pastry from a leek and potato pie she'd made the night before and wanted to use it. And blackberry pie with cream is really nice. So. He took me blackberry picking, and this was a time when he was drinking a lot, but this one day, he didn't drink, and I think it's because him and Mum had had a long talk about it the night before. I'd heard them in the kitchen with muffled voices, and it was always serious when they talked in the kitchen. They'd sit face-to-face, drinking tea and smoking, and Mum would have her elbows on the table. They wouldn't smile. Usually it was about me. But this time it wasn't, because they ended up hugging for a long time, Mum on Dad's lap, and if it had been about me, it would've ended with Dad punching a hole in the wall and thundering out of the house with Mum's screeches at his back like fingernails.

So anyway, he took me blackberry picking and he was sober and serious, and he held my hand the whole way, which I didn't mind because I was still very young and yet to grow weird about touching, and I asked him questions about blackberry picking and what you can make with blackberries, and he answered all my questions, sometimes smiling, always smoking. And we picked the blackberries, dropping them in our carrier bags, inspecting them for maggots, eating some of them, the blackberries, not the maggots, and by the time we'd finished we had purple lips and tongues, and when I poked my tongue out he smiled with real affection. But that's not the bit I focus on when I remember this day. It wasn't out of the usual for dad to be nice to me or anything. That would be painting an unfair picture. What I remember is the next bit: on the way home there was a homeless man asleep in the lane. It was quite cold out and the man's quilt had half come off. It was a dirty old quilt with yellow stains on. I didn't know how the man could sleep like that, in the cold, all exposed, but now that I'm older I know it was because of alcohol. Anyway, the blanket was only on his legs. Dad looked at me and pushed his purple finger to his lips and said, 'Shh,' and started to tiptoe over to the homeless man, and I felt a horrible feeling in my belly because I thought he was going to be mean to the man. Urinate on him or wake him up with a loud shout in the earhole. Dad could be cruel sometimes. But all he did was crouch down and bring the quilt up to the man's neck. It was such a nice and simple thing to do. I was too young to fully appreciate how kind it was back then, but now I'm a bit older, I see how most people treat homeless people. It was such a lovely day too, him being sober and calm and me not having to worry about setting off his temper, and the bowl of blackberry pie and cream at the end of it all. It's just a shame that I ruined it all.

But then, Mum should never have given me a spoon.

I don't sleep for a while. I feel too mixed up. I lie there, kicking the blankets off, pulling them back on, kicking them off again. I feel itchy on the inside, like there are germs crawling through my veins. I decide to masturbate.

Guess what?

I do it over Delyth.

Later I wake up in the dark and my dad is standing in the doorway, looking at me. Light from the hall spills out behind him. His body is a dark mass. He stands and he looks. Very still. Meditative. And then he goes away.

It might have been a dream.

The Three Rock Monsters

The print was here before Dad moved in, hung up on the wall. Dad didn't like it and I didn't like it, but we couldn't get rid of it because it belonged to the landlord and Dad was worried about losing his bond. Which is funny, considering the amount of holes he's punched in the walls and doors, and all the cannabis burns in the carpet and sofa. For a while, we left the print on my wall, but then it started to upset me, mentally, and I tucked it behind the wardrobe, where it's been ever since. It's a little bigger than the wardrobe, and its edges poke out. They make me nervous, these edges. I don't want to see any part of it. I don't want it in my room. It's like a giant spider, hiding. I keep expecting it to give me trouble. I didn't worry about this when I moved back in last week. I'd started to feel it'd lost its hold on me. An outgrown fear. But these last three days, stuck in the room while Dad drags his hooves in the darkness, it's full of its nasty old magic.

The print is one of those cheap-looking things you can buy in Ikea. Plasticky canvas stretched on a wooden frame. You usually get sunsets or panoramic views of skyscrapers or mountains. This one is a black and white landscape shot of a craggy cliff edge and rough dark water and boulders. The boulders are the main thing. They stick up out of the black water, three of them. They're rugged and grey and full of shadows and nooks. They speak of Cornwall or Fife or the Isle of Man. You can look at them and see faces – swirling, ghoulish faces, silly grinning ape faces, sinister beaky faces. But this

only happens if you look from certain angles and glaze your eyes.
I've counted thirteen different faces inside those three rocks. I used
to wake up every morning and find each face, one to thirteen. I
had a system. I kept expecting to find a fourteenth face but that
never happened.

The fourteenth face would be a terrible, terrible thing.

Each rock has a main face. A default face. The face you see
straight away without screwing your eyes up and tilting your head
like a cockatoo. The one on the left is like a dinosaur mixed in
with Marilyn Monroe. I call this one Monroe-a-saurus rex. The
one on the right is a melty old man's face. He has squinty lopsided
eyes and a fat crooked nose and he's doing that thing that cruel
children do to make fun of the mentally disabled. Tongue tucked
under bottom lip, chin bulging. Apparently it's called belming,
that thing cruel children do. But maybe someone made that up
and there is no proper word for it. Anyhow, I call this boulder
Old Belmy.

The middle boulder is the worst. It's like a dinosaur mixed with
an old bald man and it has a cluster of small boulders underneath
it which look like fingers gripping something. And the whole
thing has paunchy cheeks and a dropped-open dinosaur mouth
and a slitty snout, and it looks like it's sucking a penis in a way
that is greedy and gormless and ecstatic. Old Blowy.

One morning, a couple of years ago, I was counting the faces,
one to thirteen. I'd got to three. And then a fly landed on Old
Belmy. He stood there a while. I watched him. Or her. It's weird
thinking that flies can be girls. I thought about this while I
watched it. I wondered if girl flies have tiny vaginas, and if so,
what do they look like? And I tried to imagine what a fly's vagina
would look like, but it hurt my brain. And then the fly started to
move. It walked up Old Belmy's face and got to the top of his
craggy head. And here's the crazy part: it walked along the top of
his craggy head, following the exact edge. The *exact* edge. As if
Old Belmy was three-dimensional. Living.

And then the fly flew away.

I stood up and inspected the print closely – but not too close; it might swallow me up. So I was careful. I got out a magnifying glass from my junk box and stood a foot back, arm stretched out, hand shaking slightly. Maybe it was printed in such a way that there were raised bits, like with a painting. Maybe the fly was just following the raised ink edges.

No. Totally flat.

I put down the magnifying glass. I ducked down and quickly stroked the corner of the print, away from the rock faces, just the sea. Totally flat. I sprang back from the painting and sat on the bed, my heart going. I wiped my finger on my jeans, like there were germs on it.

The fly had shown me something. Given me a message.

The print was alive. Monroe-a-saurus rex, Old Belmy, Old Blowy, they were real and they knew things. They watched me while I slept.

They wanted me to see the fourteenth face.

I kept the picture on the wall and began to look at it more intensely than ever. It frightened me and I had trouble sleeping, but I wouldn't get rid of it, not yet. I'd sit for an hour, sometimes more, my head and body perfectly still, and stare deep into the faces of the three rock monsters. There had to be a fourteenth face. Finding it would unlock something.

One night, I was lying in the dark, arms crossed behind my head, trying to sleep. It was three in the morning. I heard Aled Mellor's garage door open out back and a swatch of light came up on my wall. It lit up the print. There were three insects on Old Belmy's head. I got out of bed and crept closer. They were crickets or grasshoppers, all the same size. They must have been young because they were as green as green beans, and with the same paradoxical texture – both silky smooth and raspy looking. They were facing each other, like a three-petal flower. Right in the middle of Old Belmy's forehead. It was like they were whispering to each other. Old Belmy's grin seemed wider than usual. Crueller. Or maybe I was tired. I looked at Old Blowy and he was the same as always. Monroe-a-saurus rex was in shadow. I heard Aled in his garage, rattling metal, clunking things about. I wondered what he was doing in his garage at three in the morning. I looked at the grasshoppers again. They had long antennae. I'd never seen grasshoppers so vibrant.

Aled turned off his garage light and my wall went dark. This was just after a time Dad scraped the glitter off my light switch over an argument. I rushed toward my bedroom door and opened it. The hall light was on. Its haze spilled into my room, softening the darkness. I looked at Old Belmy. The green-bean crickets were gone.

The next morning I went a little crazy. The three crickets were a sign, a message. It all came back to the number three, I figured. Three rocks, three crickets. I'd counted three faces when the fly showed up that time. It was three in the morning with the crickets. So three was important.

As soon as I woke up I decided I would blink three times before and after everything I did. I blinked three times. I got out of bed. Blinked three times. Sat on the edge of the bed. Blinked three times. I looked at the print. Blinked three times. I counted thirteen faces, blinked three times. Counted thirteen faces again, blinked three times. I repeated this. Three lots of counting. System within a system. I masturbated. I did it in strokes of three – up down, up down, up down, pause. Repeat. I imagined Kate Bush with three breasts and three heads and three vaginas and three sets of red pillow lips. Me with three penises. Ridiculous. I used three antibacterial wipes to clean myself.

The whole day, like this. Instead of eating a banana I'd eat three bananas. When walking I took three steps, paused, blinked three times, took another three steps, and so on. It was challenging. I was getting a headache. I took three paracetamol. Not good for the kidneys. And I only had two kidneys. But that wasn't my fault.

I wanted to stop. It was getting like Patty with her spear bones and her sevens. But I felt I was close to unlocking something. I decided I would continue until three o'clock in the morning. And at three o'clock exactly I would blink three times and look at Old Belmy, because this was all down to him, not the others, he was the powerful one, and I was guessing that at three o'clock exactly I would find the fourteenth face, which was what all this was about. That's what the crickets and the fly had been trying to tell me. But I had to do it right. So I went on with the triple blinking, and I had dinner at three in the afternoon, eating three slices of rye bread with hummus blobbed on top, and when I felt a fart coming, I held it in, because I couldn't be sure it would come out times three, or for three seconds, and the gas built up in my stomach, which isn't surprising, the amount of fibre I eat, and it got painful, so I looked at the time and saw it was ten minutes to six, and I waited until it was three minutes to six exactly and let out the gas, which came out in two long, odourless hisses, so I'd been right to play it safe.

Before bed I asked Dad to put my light on for me, because I'd need to be able to see Old Belmy's face (though I didn't tell him that), and he did it without question because he was feeling guilty about scraping my glitter off. I worried a while because he hadn't pressed the light switch three times. And that might mess everything up. But then I figured that the law of threes only applied to me – I had no control over what other people did, just as I had no control over how many kidneys I had.

Honestly, it was crazy. It was like the part of me that works against myself and causes all the trouble, the OCD part, had got hold of my logic and kidnapped it, and now my logic was lying inside a locked-up trunk, squirming in the dark and crying out with tied-up wrists and ankles.

But it was also divine. There is a peculiar euphoria that comes from making these rules within these worlds. It's a comforting feeling and a powerful one. It's like being a child, a little dictatorial child willingly locked within the walls of infinite imagination.

I lay on my bed until three o'clock. A moth flew into my room and flapped erratically around the light bulb, plinking into it. Another sign. 'It's good that you have the light on at this hour,' it told me. 'You're on the right track, soon all will be revealed to you.' I wondered what the fourteenth face would look like. Monstrous, probably. Rotten, skeletal, melty. Something that's been dead a while.

It got to three o'clock.

I blinked three times and looked at Old Belmy.

He grinned back.

I stared for three minutes.

Nothing.

I got up and pulled the print off the wall and shoved it behind the wardrobe.

I blinked four times.

Incidentally, it hadn't been Aled Mellor in his garage that time. It'd been burglars, and they'd stolen his bicycle, his lawnmower and his toolkit. He'd blamed Dad for it, and the police had come round the flat to ask questions. And that's why Dad defecated in Aled's ornamental well.

Now. I pull the print out from behind the wardrobe with nervous fingers and lean it against the wall. There they are – Old Belmy, Old Blowy and Monroe-a-saurus rex. Old Blowy is as ridiculous and grotesque as he always was. Old Belmy just as nasty. Monroe-a-saurus though, she's changed. There's a dusty, fluffy cobweb stretched across her face like a mourning veil. I don't see a spider. Maybe she swallowed it up. A long tongue suddenly flicking out from the canvas, snatching it. No. No. Ridiculous. Probably it just moved somewhere else because it wasn't catching enough flies. Logic.

It's hot in my room. I can smell concentrated urine coming through my window. I can't hear Dad. Maybe he's still asleep. I lie back on my bed, arms crossed behind my head, and find the thirteen faces.

I can always sense when my thinking is getting dangerous. Some days, when I'm feeling in control, I stop it at an early point. Nip it in the bud, my dad would say. Other days I let it happen. Fudge it, I think. 'Fudge it' is what my mum used to say when I was in the room and she didn't want to swear. And 'flipping hell' and 'oh flip' and 'oh bum'.

I've been looking for the fourteenth face. For a sign.

Dad wakes up around noon. I hear him cough his man's lungy cough and thud through the hall. He goes into the bathroom to use the toilet, flushes. His electric shaver comes on and I imagine him tilting his chin with his lips pulled down at the sides. Screwing on attachments so he can do his nostrils and ears. He's a hairy man, my dad. Curly grey hairs all over, some bits thick, some bits sparse. Except his shins. They're shiny bald. I'm not hairy at all, except for my armpits and testicles and anus, and even this hairiness is a fluffy blond hairiness. I don't need to shave my face. Which is lucky, because I'd turn it into a ritual skin flaying.

Dad turns the shaver off and goes down the hall again. He stops outside my door. My heart thumps against my breast like a frozen hambone. I sit rigid, my eyes stuck on Old Belmy's spiteful crags. Then Dad carries on to the living room.

I need to get out, I think. I should leave now. Or should I?

I need a sign.

Jeremy Beadle is Sacrificed to the Beast

The day just drips away when you're in a state of conviction. I've been slow-staring at Old Belmy for hours, only moving to eat some trail mix and take some diclofenac. By the time the streetlights have come on I've mostly given up. But that's often the way with epiphanies.

It's dark and I'm lying on my bed. I hear my dad opening the back door and I think, having a beer in the garden, probably, and I worry that he'll smell my condensed urine out there, but then I think, so what? And I scratch my nose and look at the dark canvas and it comes, the epiphany, it sneaks up on me.

If I turn the print upside down, there will be new faces.

So simple.

My stomach fills with flutters. So simple. I'll see the fourteenth face straight away. And then I'll know what to do.

My eyes move to the light switch. It's a dark smudge. Maybe I can just do it quickly, with an elbow, I think. Or my forehead or nose, like people do when their hands are full with cups of tea and plates of toast. I don't even have to look at it. A quick elbow stab, eyes closed. And if I get drawn in, so what?

I'm already going crazy. What's one light switch?

Maybe, in fact, the light switch is necessary.

Maybe the light switch patterns were never about keeping Bad Things away. Maybe they were codes. Codes to unlock the Fourteenth Face.

I stand up. Walk toward the switch.

Then I hear it. A noise out in the garden. A scuffling, a banging. Foxes, I think. You get foxes in the area sometimes. You find them dead by the side of the road, and it's sad because they look so precious and complete.

I look out of the window, and there's Dad in his boxers, just his boxers, dragging Aled Mellor over the fence by his hair and his clothes. One hand bunched in the hair, one in the lapel of his dressing gown. Dragging him over. Dad looks silvery pale in the darkness. His belly glistens like an eyeball. Aled is groaning through his teeth. I can hear him. It must hurt, getting scraped over a fence like that. I can smell my urine through the open window.

Dad pulls Aled all the way over and Aled lands on the grass in a mewling sprawl, his skinny white legs all askew, his dressing gown rucked up to show his underpants. Dad kicks him in the ribs. Aled woodlouse-rolls into a ball and twitches. Dad kneels down and straddles Aled and starts pounding his head.

And I'm just watching from the window, breathing through my mouth.

Dad stops. He looks tired. His shoulders slump. He presses a palm against Aled's cheek, holds it there, breathing hard. I don't know what Aled's doing. I can see his wormy white legs sticking out, his underpants, his arm, but not his face. He could be unconscious. Or dead. Dad leaves his hand on Aled's cheek. He's hunched over him like a goblin.

And I'm just watching. From the window. Breathing through my mouth.

Dad gets up off Aled. He stumbles with loose legs over to the patio chair, but doesn't sit. Stands there, looking at the knuckles on his right hand, shoulders still slumped. Aled lies there, still. On his back. If I squint I can see his tiny shrunken hand with its jelly bean fingers. Then his leg twitches, once, twice, three times.

There's my sign.

I take my pyjama bottoms off and put on a pair of jeans. My room is dark but I can see enough. I put them on, then some shoes, no socks. I grab a shirt that's draped over the back of my chair. I stand in the middle of the room and run my hands through my greasy hair. What do I need to take? What do I need?

I go back to the window. Aled's still on the ground, motionless. Dad's swaying a little. I think he's wet himself. He's looking down at the grass. He curls his feet into the grass. Scratches his testicles. It feels like I'm watching a nature documentary, something shot at night with one of those special cameras, and Aled is a dead antelope, and Dad is a bear, a giant grizzly bear who is ambling around post-kill, sniffing things, licking blood off his claws, satisfied. I know bears don't kill antelopes, usually lions do, or tigers, but Dad would never be a lion or a tiger. Always the bear or the bull.

Dad seems to come out of his daze. He looks at Aled. Stares at him a while, his cheeks slack, his hair spirit white in the moonlight. He looks down at his toes in the grass. Curls them again. He puts both hands on his big belly, spreads his fingers and squeezes. And then he looks up.

He looks up at me.

And I'm watching from the window. Breathing through my mouth.

He frowns. All sorts of things are happening in his brain, thoughts, connections, ideas, fears. I can see them all forming, swimming together through the drunken swamp.

'You,' he says.

He takes a step forward, his belly jiggling. I take a step back. 'Wait,' he says, taking another step. He looks confused.

I'm not confused. I know exactly what to do.

I snatch Dad's wallet from the coffee table on the way out.

Batshit

I don't stop running till I'm three streets away. Even then, I walk fast, looking back over my shoulder for Dad. Dad in his underpants, running down the road, blood on his knuckles. Shouting 'Come back, come back!', like he did the time he broke my nose. But not this time.

So what is he doing?

I come up with five options:

He's trying to wake up Aled but Aled won't wake up. Because Aled is dead. So he sits on the grass in frozen silence for a while, not knowing what to do. And, eventually, he either drags Aled into the house and rings up someone for help, one of his gangster friends, or he leaves Aled out in the garden. It's also possible that Aled's silent mouse-wife comes out into the garden looking for her husband, calling his name, and Dad panics and drags Aled into the house superfast, getting grass stains on his poor white pants.

Or… He wakes up Aled and sort of pats his shoulder and apologises, though at the same time making it clear that Aled is also at fault. 'Silly, ain't it, us two fighting like this?' he says, choosing his words carefully. Dad can rewrite history with that one word, 'fighting'. He says it in a voice which is intimidating and kind at the same time, wavering between both – a sly guilt. Aled is stupefied with concussion, his head bobbing. Dad helps him to his feet and leads him through the house, out the front door. 'Get some ice on that,' he says, and Aled nods, his jaw slack, before traipsing across the front lawn and going back into his own house.

Or… The same as above, but Aled is not dazed and confused, he's furious. He gets up off the grass, ready to call the police, wincing because his ribs are broken and his head is hurting, and Dad says, in a quiet, dreadful voice, 'You want to think very carefully about your next move, Al.' And Aled stops and looks at my dad, meeting his eye, and he pulls a disgusted face and says, 'You're threatening me,' and Dad nods, his face in shadow, and says, 'Correct.'

Or. Aled doesn't wake up, but Aled isn't dead. There's blood dripping out of his ear but he's breathing. Dad calls an ambulance.

Or… The same as above, but Dad doesn't call an ambulance. Instead he cups a hand over Aled's mouth and nose and squeezes, cutting off the man's air. And Aled dies. He drags Aled into the house, getting grass stains on his poor white pants, and he leaves him on the kitchen floor then sits on the recycling bin, drinking beer and thinking about who to call and what to do about the wife.

After about ten minutes I stop under a lamp post. I'm still breathing through my mouth. I don't know why – my nose isn't blocked or anything. I pull Dad's wallet out of my breast pocket. Two hundred and forty pounds in crisp twenties. I count it three times, just to make sure.

I could go to a hotel in the city centre, one with a little fridge stocked with alcohol I won't drink, a big TV with Sky, room service, nice food, and they won't mind me being particular with my requests because they're probably used to vegans and Americans and people with allergies. I could treat myself. Or I could go to Patty's. She's very honest and full of solid advice, and she probably doesn't even remember that time in the park.

Really, it's awful that I'm thinking of myself right now. With

Aled lying in the garden, his underpants showing. Mum always said that unwell people are selfish. And she knew all about it because her sister had clinical depression, and when Mum phoned her once a week, on Sunday, Aunt Belinda would only ever talk about her miserable self, never asking how her sister was doing, and even after Mum was diagnosed, Aunt Belinda would only focus on that for two minutes before swinging the conversation back to herself. 'She thinks she's under the blinkin' bell jar,' Mum would say, and I didn't understand that because I was too young for Sylvia Plath, I just thought Mum was making a joke about her sister's name. 'She's completely and utterly self-absorbed.' And then she'd ruffle my hair, which I didn't mind because I never got weird about my mum touching me, never, and she'd say, 'People, eh? Can't live with 'em, can't murder 'em.'

That was her sense of humour.

It was me thinking I was psychic that caused all the trouble with Dad that time. The time with the broken nose.

It was a year ago and I was almost seventeen. Mum had been gone three years. Old Belmy and his friends had been living behind the wardrobe for a couple of months now. I wanted to look at the canvas, like an itch, but I stayed strong. Because it would be one of those strange, deep foot itches that you can't find to scratch. That's how my counsellor at the time, Tim, explained it to me. He'd tried to convince me to throw the print away, and 'bugger the landlord'. A few quid is nothing when it comes to your mental health, he told me. But I refused because I had this noble idea that keeping it there behind the wardrobe was a good way of exercising my willpower and strength.

Anyway. This one morning I saw a dead pigeon in the street. It was the day Amy Winehouse died. Amy and the pigeon – were their deaths linked? Maggots were fidgeting around in the pigeon's eye sockets. This had to mean something. Across the road from the dead pigeon there was a soggy newspaper in the gutter with its pages all strewn. And if I read that newspaper in a certain way, I'd find out what it all meant. The maggots would be behind it, definitely. I crossed the road to look at the newspaper and a girl on a bicycle almost crashed into me. She veered just in time and righted herself, shouting, 'Look where you're going!' It was a sign. It told me to ignore the newspaper sign because that was the wrong sign. It was a sign within a sign.

No, I decided. This is all crazy thinking. And I went home. I went home and I thought about the film, *A Beautiful Mind*, which is about the mathematical genius and code cracker John Nash, who was schizophrenic. I thought, I'm starting to think like him. I'm becoming like him. But without the beautiful. Maybe it was schizophrenia, me thinking all these strange things and looking for signs all the time. It was going beyond magical thinking.

I didn't sleep at all that night. I didn't even masturbate. I lay in my bed with glimmering eyes, worrying my stomach into a walnut.

It all got a lot worse the following week.

I was out walking and listening to my portable DAB radio. I can't remember what channel I was tuned into, but it was probably 6 Music or Radio 2. Anyway, the DJ, a man, was talking to a woman on the phone, and she was telling him how she did gigs around pubs in her area, singing the songs of female artists from the sixties, and he asked her who her favourite artist was to sing, and Peggy Lee came into my head. Just came out of nowhere like a light bulb ping. And a second later, guess what the woman said.

She said Peggy Lee.

I stopped walking. I was near Maindy Barracks. There was a man walking a fat Labrador ahead of me. There was no good reason for me to guess Peggy Lee. It wasn't like Peggy Lee encapsulated the sixties.

I carried on walking. I remembered the time I first heard that

Hadouken! song, 'That Boy That Girl', and there was that bit in it where he sang, 'All the band boys with your special beakers,' and I'd flown into a frenzy, thinking it was a sign, because how many boys have special beakers? And I'd listened to it over and over, trying to decipher the message – 'What's a band boy? Am I a band boy? Maybe it's "banned" instead of "band". Hasn't my OCD banned me from life?' Then I'd googled the lyrics and it was 'specs and sneakers', not 'special beakers', and I calmed down a bit.

But this was different. I walked and I wondered if schizophrenic people really were crazy – they could just be more highly tuned into the world. Seeing and hearing things other people can't or won't, like dogs and cats and small children. Maybe they're psychic.

Maybe I was psychic.

The next day I was in the kitchen, drinking some lychee juice. From my special beaker. Dad came in wearing only a pair of grey jogging bottoms. He was rubbing his big hairy belly and yawning all stretchy-jawed with a white tongue showing. He went over to the radio and turned it on. In the second it took for the music to come on, I thought to myself, in that wordless, disjointed way people think to themselves, that I'd love to hear some Björk, and wouldn't it be good if a Björk song was playing right now? The music came on. Guess what?

Björk. 'Human Behaviour'.

'What's wrong with you?' my dad said. 'You look like you need a massive shit all of a sudden.'

'Have you ever wondered if you're psychic?' I blurted out.

He frowned, hands back on his belly. Fingers splayed, the grey hairs sticking through the gaps. 'No, Sylvester. Because I am sane.'

I looked down at my lychee juice. There were little bits floating in it.

'What's happening inside that head of yours, Sylv?'

'Nothing.'

97

'You think you're psychic, don't you?'

'No, it's just—'

'What am I thinking?'

'What?'

'What am I thinking?'

I stared at the floaty bits. As if they could tell me what to say. Maybe they could. 'I don't know.'

'Ex-fucking-zactly.' He came over to me and tilted my chin up with one finger. His hands smelled meaty. 'You are not psychic.'

I nodded. He nodded.

'There's no such thing,' he said.

'I know it,' I said.

'Ex-fucking-zactly.'

It had something to do with electromagnetism, I reckoned. I was tuned into a higher frequency. Or a *different* frequency; let's not be narcissistic. I wasn't sure if it was a spiritual or scientific thing. I thought about it for hours, lying on my bed as usual, looking for connections – as usual. It could be aliens. I looked at the edge of the print poking out from behind my wardrobe. It could have something to do with the Fourteenth Face.

I went to my PC and opened up a new Notepad document.

'Björk and Peggy Lee,' I wrote. 'Aliens?'

It was easy with Björk. The clues were in her songs: 'Earth Intruders', 'Human Behaviour'. And she was such an oddity. I didn't know much about Peggy Lee, and she was dead.

But alive in another dimension?

I wanted to get the picture out from behind the wardrobe. 'I'm already thinking crazy things,' I thought. 'What's another crazy thing on top of the pile?' I looked at the edges of the print. 'In for a penny, in for a pound,' I thought. But that was just my OCD sitting like a plump red devil on my shoulder. It was like when alcoholics find excuses to drink. It's the illness doing it. Maybe

I'm not too far gone, I thought. I could snap out of this. Straighten out all the curls and kinks and spirals in my mind with sheer will. I'd stumbled across some interesting coincidences, that was all. Aliens? Psychic? Really, Skillacorn? *Really?*

I stared at the wall. It was clean and unstained. Pure white.

I turned back to the screen and typed 'Peggy Lee songs lyrics' into the search bar.

'Did I ever tell you about Debbie the Bike and her mother,' my dad said.

We were in the back garden. This was the day after the Björk song came on the radio; I was sleep deprived and fidgety. It wasn't sunny or even warm, but we were sat there in the patio chairs because workmen were inside the house making lots of noise. Dad was drinking beer. He was drunk.

I shook my head.

'Debbie the Bike was my girlfriend back when I was sixteen,' he said. 'She was a bit of a girl.' He lit a cigarette and tucked the lighter back in his jacket pocket. 'Her mother was a fortune teller. She dressed up like a Romany and told fortunes in the indoor market. Bunch of bollocks, I thought. Just exploiting stupid people. She wasn't even a Romany. She came from Pontardawe.'

He tapped some ash onto the grass. A great crashing sound came from inside the house. He winced. 'Fucking brutes,' he said. 'They break anything and I'll break their legs.' The kitchen units were being replaced. The workmen had been round for two days. They didn't use coasters.

'Anyway,' he said. 'I was around Debbie's one night and I went down to the kitchen for some beer, and the mother was there, all decked out in her gyppo clothes. She'd just come home from work. If you can call it that.' He smirked. 'She was taking off her rings. All these big silver rings, loads of them. She grabbed me as I was getting the beer out of the fridge and I thought, "Oh shit," like maybe she thought I was rude going in the fridge like that, ya know? Even though Debbie'd said it was OK. And there was also a part of me that thought she was going to come on to me. Because that'd happened before with the mother of another girlfriend.' He winked. 'Anyway. She grabs me and looks into my eyes. She's got all this black eyeliner on and it's in the creases of her eyes, cuz she's old. About forty. Although that's not really old.' A small shrug. 'But I was only sixteen.'

Another crash came from the house, but this time Dad ignored it.

'She stared into my eyes. And I'll never forget what she said to me. She says, "You're going to have a son. A blond son. But it won't be with Debbie." She said it in her normal accent, and all matter-of-fact. Not like the BS she gave her customers. "You'll be married, but it'll end. I don't see any other children, just a son. He'll be difficult."'

I stared at him.

'Aye, difficult,' said Dad. 'And the rest.'

'She was right,' I said. 'About all of it.'

He nodded. 'She also told me not to waste any time on her daughter. "I love her but she's loose," she said. "Sad but true." And it was. She shagged some boy who worked in the cake factory a few weeks later. She wasn't called a bike for nothing.' He pointed a finger at me and raised his brows. 'Funny though. I found her on Facebook recently. She's with a woman now. So now she's Debbie the Dyke.'

He looked at me with expectance, his eyes crinkling and twinkling.

'Why are you telling me this?' I said.

He brought the beer to his lips, pausing to say, 'Wassat?'

'I thought you said that there's no such thing?'

'Eh?'

'Being psychic. You said there's no such thing. But she was right about everything.'

He knitted his eyebrows. 'Maybe there isn't. Maybe there is. We'll never know.' He looked at me. 'So don't waste your time thinking about it. The world is full of mysteries, and that's not about to change.' He crushed his cigarette out on the patio table. 'You've been spending too much time alone in your bedroom lately.'

'I'm fine,' I said.

'Are you?'

I nodded.

'Have you spoken to the doctor about going on meds like they talked about?'

I shook my head.

'Perhaps you should.'

I stared at him again. Dad didn't believe in taking meds for anything, 'except serious loony tunes shit'. He felt that most mentally ill people just had too much time on their hands.

'No, I don't want to,' I said.

'OK, OK, your choice,' he said. He stuck his chin in and burped. 'Let me tell you another story.'

I smiled. I liked my dad's stories.

'When your mum was pregnant, this was. Eight months gone, something like that.' He stuck his free hand out over his belly. 'Out here, she was. Huge.' He burped again. It smelled like curry. 'Anyway, we had these cats at the time. Kittens, more like. Two brothers, Kuato and Murder Death Kill. Named by yours truly, obviously. Little shits, they were, always bringing in dead things or dying things. It really upset your mother. And then this one morning, we woke up, and there's three dead baby birds downstairs. One in the living room, two in the kitchen. Except they weren't dead, but near enough.' He lit a fresh cigarette. 'The cats hadn't done much to them, but they'd been taken from the nest and they were so young. Bald mostly, just a couple of tiny feathers. But your mother, she wanted to save them.' He smiled. 'You know what she was like. Remember those vegetarian lasagnes she used to cook?' He scrunched his mouth up. 'Horrible. But we never said anything, did we?'

I shook my head.

'So anyway. She wanted to save these dying birds, bless her, so she put them in Tupperware boxes near a radiator, to keep them warm, and she tried to feed them milk. Which is not what you feed a dying bird, but of course, we didn't have the internet back then to guide us, so we were playing it by ear. I say "we", but really it was her. I was just going about my business, you know.

'It took two hours for the first bird to die. Then another couple of hours for the next one. Then there was only one left, and your mum, she thought it was a fighter. It was the plumpest, see, and it took the milk she gave it. "Susan," I says, "don't get your hopes up. It's been taken from the nest too young. It'll die of shock like the others." But she wouldn't have it, would she? "You are always so *negative*," she says. "You never know, you just never know." But I knew. It was sad watching it all. The bird was a goner, but she wouldn't have it. Kept on with the milk. And you know what happened?' He looked at me. 'She drowned it. Drowned it with milk. It died in her palm, its throat all blocked up with semi-skimmed. Puking it up. We were out the garden, having a barbeque. Couple of friends over, you know. And the bird died, and she watched it die and she got so upset. She didn't cry or nothing, because deep down, she'd known it was a goner anyway, with or without milk, with or without hope and fucking positivity. And we buried it while the chicken wings were cooking. Fucking symbolic, eh? And she said a little prayer in a sarky way, like it didn't matter, but really she was gutted, I could tell. And after, I couldn't eat my chicken wings.'

He smiled at me with an expression I couldn't read. Drank some more beer, smoked his cigarette. 'But anyway. There's a point to this story. There is a point.'

'Which you're going to get to next Christmas,' I said, but smiling.

'Gobshite,' he said, smoke seeping out of his nose. But smiling. 'Now bear in mind that your mum was heavily pregnant at this time. And she was scared about everything – about the birth, about whether she'd be a good mother, about me – whether I'd start using again, if I'd be a good dad or a bad dad. You know. And the day the birds died, she got *extra* scared. She freaked out a bit. Because she'd drowned that last one with milk. Talk about symbolism!' He shook his head. 'That's not what a pregnant woman needs, that kind of shit. And course, she was a thinker, like you. Like me, after too much time with Vera.' He nodded, hands back on his stomach. 'Yes, I'm like it too, sometimes. An *over*-thinker. And she got it into her head that it was a premonition. A sign.'

I started at that. And he saw. He tipped his eyebrows slyly. 'I see I have struck a nerve.'

I looked down at my lap. He reached across and laid a cold hand on my wrist. 'You see? I know you. I know my son.'

I looked up at him, wrist tingling. 'So you think Mum had OCD?'

He screwed his face up. 'No! You're missing the point. She didn't have OCD. She was just scared like everyone else and she read too much into things sometimes. Not everything needs a label, Sylv.'

'But I have OCD,' I said.

He nodded, his cheeks full of beer. Swallowed. 'Aye. *You* have OCD. You most certainly do.'

'But everyone has the seeds of it,' I said, reiterating what I'd been told time and again by professionals.

'Yes. We all have the seeds, son. But it only turns into OCD if you indulge it. And your mother, she didn't indulge it. She got over it. And look – she gave birth to a healthy baby and she was a wonderful mum.'

'You make it sound easy,' I said.

He shrugged. 'Maybe. Maybe I know fuck all.' He tilted his bottle at me. 'But I know *you*. I know my son. And I know you're driving yourself batshit.'

And with that, he stood up, let out a long, guttural burp, ruffled my hair, and went back inside to argue with the builders.

There was a red balloon. This was a few days later. A red balloon. It was floating up over the houses in Africa Gardens. I was walking home from school. I was studying A-levels in English Lit and Chemistry and Biology, but I hardly ever showed up for class because every morning I was having to fight a panic attack. Standing in the middle of my bedroom in my socks and underpants whispering 'timolol' to myself in an oxygen-choked voice, eyes closed, the smell of bacon drifting up from the kitchen.

It didn't matter that the balloon was red. It meant nothing. It certainly didn't mean danger or blood or stop. I wouldn't indulge it. I watched it float over the useless chimneys and then I stopped looking. I told myself a story about a young blond motherless boy who gets food poisoning from eating roast beef, and how it's karma because he's supposed to be a vegetarian, and it's a special kind of food poisoning and his vomit comes out like thousands of tiny skulls and he grows hooves, and the only way he can redeem himself and stop the poison is to save the lives of twenty cows (certainly not fourteen), which he does.

I reached my street. The young motherless boy had managed to rescue twenty cows from a slaughterhouse and his hooves were turning back into hands, so it was good timing. I got to the flat. And guess what?

There was the red balloon. Floating just by Dad's front door. It had a number seven on it.

Of all the houses in all the streets.

This isn't fair, I thought. I'd been trying so hard to think clear. I'd thought up that story with all the details, all the small details, like how the young blond motherless boy had one iris just slightly bigger than the other and how his favourite food in the world was grilled courgettes, only he liked them slightly burnt at the edges – all these details. And now this had happened. It wasn't fair.

And the worst thing?

My dad's house number is two.

And seven times two equals fourteen.

Dad usually knocked before he came into my room because once he'd caught me masturbating. He didn't this time. The door swung open and there he was, blocking the doorway, his eyes hard blue.

He looked at the balloon in my hands. It was shrivelled up now. Saggy fingermarks denting the surface.

'Where d'you get that?'

I looked at the balloon as if I was surprised to find myself holding it. 'This? Um. Outside.'

He closed his eyes in a huffy way, opened them. 'Sylvester. You've been in this room for three days. You haven't showered and you haven't slept. I know this because I can fucking hear you. Playing fucking music. All fucking night.'

It was true. I'd stayed up analysing Amy Winehouse.

'Look at you. You look like a ghost.'

Also true. I was pale and I had the eyes of a scared rat. I'd got to that stage of sleeplessness where I kept seeing things out of the corner of my eye. Twitchy things. The ghosts of all the spiders I'd ever stepped on.

'If you're driving yourself batshit over something, I'd like to know,' said Dad.

I just stared at the red balloon. Batshit. How had the word 'batshit' come to mean crazy? How had it happened? Language was so strange.

Dad came over and snatched the balloon out of my hands. It made a rubbery squeak as it left my fingers.

'Sylvester! Talk to me.'

I glanced up at him. I had this overwhelming urge to say, 'I see dead people,' in a hoarse whisper, and the idea made me giggle. It was a queer sort of giggle. I must have looked like a lunatic. Batshit.

'Right,' said Dad. He grabbed me roughly by the arm and yanked me up. 'You're coming to the doctors with me.'

'No!'

'Yes! You're coming to the doctors and you're going to take whatever they give you. Because you're not *well*, Sylvester.'

I ripped my arm loose of his grip. 'I'm fine!'

He wrapped his hand around the back of my neck and pulled me close. 'You're not.' I could smell beer on his breath.

I was scared. I pushed him, hard. It was kind of like a strike too, because it hurt my wrists. He stumbled back a couple of steps. He looked at me. There is a look in someone's eye that tells you they are going to hit you. It's a very brief flash. You see it but you don't have time to think about it. Because then they hit you.

It was my nose he went for.

My blood burst over the carpet and over my clothes. I fell onto my back. Blood was dripping over my lips and into my mouth. Dad stood there looking at me. There is a look in someone's eyes when they realise they've done a bad thing. It's a slow, gradual fade like colour pouring out of the skin when all the oxygen has gone. Dad's shoulders slumped. He still had the balloon in his hand.

Red for danger.

There was an ad on Gumtree. 'Housemate wanted.' It was Keith. He was a 'tidy and solitary smoker', looking for similar. No pets. His original housemate had just moved out and he needed a replacement, someone who'd help pay the rent. Or who would get the government to help pay the rent. I replied to his ad and he invited me over. It was a two-bedroom terraced house with frayed carpets and mould in the bathroom, but I didn't care about any of that. I just wanted to get away from Dad. Keith seemed quiet and miserable, but I didn't care about that either. I'd be spending most of my time in the bedroom. I told him this and he nodded with a face all blank and sallow. 'Well, whatever. It's yours if you want it.' I told him I did.

106

What I didn't tell him was that I'd be needing the toilet and hall lights kept on every night or, alternatively, if this wasn't acceptable, glitter glue on all the light switches.

'What happened to your nose?' he asked me.

'Someone punched me,' I said.

'Fair enough.'

He led me into the kitchen so we could discuss business. The name of the estate agent was David Winters. Winters was my mother's maiden name. Which meant nothing. This was a fresh start.

The social didn't want to pay for my housing because I was under eighteen and still under my father's care. I had to say I was estranged from him. Which was only half true, because we were on speaking terms still. Sort of. After he'd broken my nose, I'd run from the house and Dad had chased me, yelling 'Come back!' and he caught up with me, because I wanted him to catch up with me, and then he'd apologised with eyes drooping guiltily and driven me to the hospital. I was too shell-shocked to care that he was drunk. I just sat there staring at the licence plates of the cars in front, not even forming words. He drove, eyes locked on the road. He was probably thinking of Mum. Remembering how she used to get when he Let The Bull Out.

We sat in A&E on those hard plastic chairs, waiting. He drank coffee and jiggled his leg, and sometimes his thigh touched against mine and I stiffened and he noticed.

I didn't look for any signs in that waiting room. The broken-armed young boy opposite me was wearing a red T-shirt. *And* he was blond. I could have had a field day with that.

It was almost as if Dad had knocked some sense into me.

The doctor who examined my nose was a young Indian woman called Dr Chakraborty, which I thought was a wonderful name. She asked me what had happened and I said, 'I got punched,' at the same time as Dad said, 'He fell over.' That was awkward. Dr

Chakraborty's eyes flicked from my face to Dad's face and back again. She looked tiredly cynical but kind at the same time. 'Will you be wanting to involve the police?' she asked.

I sensed my dad stiffen up next to me.

'I just want my nose fixed,' I said. 'It hurts.'

'Are you sure?' she said.

'Yes,' I said. 'It hurts a lot.'

The Pied Biker of Pontcanna

It's been half an hour since Dad killed Aled. *Hurt* Aled. I'm near the old bridge where a student got run over a month ago. Across the road there's a lamp post with a shrunken bunch of flowers at the bottom.

Will Aled Mellor get flowers outside his house?

And my dad. What will he get?

'Shut up,' I whisper. Because Aled is fine, absolutely fine.

When I get to town there's lots of people, drunk people. They're climbing into taxis or shouting or whooping or eating chips in squirrel-eyed huddles. What day is it? Wednesday, Thursday? It must be a student night. It can't be Friday already. A little further up, on the steps of the museum, there's a man with a guitar and a few people sitting around him. He's playing 'American Pie'. I sit a few steps above. The guitar player is a skinny man in a denim jacket. Sat in front of him is a woman who looks homeless, her hair all dreadlocked into a big brown clump. Then there's a black man with a can of alcohol in his hand. Next to him are two girls a little older than me. One of them is pretty and one of them is beautiful. The pretty one has long red hair and pale skin, and the beautiful one is mixed race with long black straightened hair and large eyes under roofs of thick lazy lashes. Both are wearing dresses and have naked legs, nice legs.

'American Pie' finally comes to an end. 'Yow know any Beatles?'

the homeless woman says in a witchy, Birmingham accent. She's got some teeth missing.

'"Hey Jude"?' says the guitar player.

They all clap and make noises. Except the black man. He's looking at the beautiful girl's breasts. They're average-sized and very round. He edges a little closer to her, tipping his drink, and presses his knee against her knee. She doesn't notice. She's rolling a cigarette. Her nails are painted red. Which means nothing.

The guitar player gets some bits wrong and has to start again. The homeless woman joins in with the singing. She closes her eyes and tilts her head and her mouth resembles a baby's mouth. I watch the beautiful one seal her Rizla, tongue tip flicking out from between her soft lips, sliding slowly along the paper's gummy strip. She rolls the cigarette between her red-tipped fingers, the red meaning nothing, absolutely nothing – let's get that clear right now: *nothing* – and picks out a fluff of tobacco. She lights it, blows out smoke and glances at me. I look away.

I think of Aled Mellor's little jelly bean finger.

I really should call 999. Maybe it's not too late.

'Ey, you. Blondie.'

It's the beautiful girl. She's looking at me with smoke coming out of her nose.

'Come over here, Blondie. Sit with us.'

I go over to them, thinking maybe one of them has a phone so I can call 999.

But deep, deep down, deep in the wheezing bowels of my belly, I know that I'm not going to make that call.

Sorry Mr Mellor. Sorry about your underpants. I don't think I'm your man.

He plays 'Layla' next, by the Kinks. Everyone loves this one. And the beautiful girl is smiling at me. With those soft, soft lips. Which are a dark pink stretching into lilac. And even though I have a low self-esteem sometimes, and my penis is dysfunctional,

I know I'm reasonably good looking. Not just because my mum always said it, and Patty says it and Jenny my first and only girlfriend used to say it. But because my dad once said it. Reluctantly. Sandwiched between two insults.

But I don't want to think about Dad.

So the girl. The beautiful girl. She smiles at me. The black man is looking at me with slurring mistrust. He's skinny with big eyes and his hair is halfway between Afro and curly. He's very drunk and his head is bobbing a little. Now that I'm closer I can see that he's drinking Special Brew lager, which is very strong and disgusting, according to Patty. The homeless woman is also drinking Special Brew, and she sips it in between verses and choruses. Her big clumpy dreadlock is the colour of dried mud.

The guitar player finishes 'Layla'. He tunes his guitar and then plucks the strings mindlessly, humming to himself. The black man leans even closer to the beautiful girl. He puts his hand on her thigh and laughs.

'You must come home with me, girl of my heart,' he says in a strong African accent.

The beautiful girl pushes his hand off her leg. 'I'm a lesbian.'

She glances at me when she says this. She's not a lesbian.

'What is this?'

'Lesbian,' she says, shrinking back from him. 'I'm a lesbian. A rug-muncher.'

Her pretty friend reaches over and takes her hand. 'Leave my girlfriend alone.'

The black man grins. 'Ah! Lesbian-ah, sweet lesbian-ah. Comes down from the sky-ah.' He looks up at the sky, his face upturned. Stretches his arms, the Special Brew dribbling down his wrist. The pretty one leans over and spits into his can. He doesn't notice. 'Sweet, sweet lesbian-ah, come down from the sky-ah!' He shakes his head like he cannot believe what the world is coming to, and drinks.

The two girls huddle over laughing.

It's a mean thing to do, I think, spitting in his drink like that. A high school thing to do.

All the same. She smiles at me again, the beautiful one. Soft, soft lips, stretching into lilac. And I forgive her.

How easy it is to do that.

The black man wanders off, stumbling and chattering to himself. He's got some sort of gungy liquid on the seat of his trousers and I feel sorry for him.

A grinning man on a bicycle comes up to us. He's got long blond dreadlocks and he's skinny. He's got the kind of face where you're reminded of the skull under the skin.

'You gorgeous thing,' he says to the homeless woman. 'How are you enjoying this fine evening?' He has a clear voice with no obvious accent.

The homeless woman smiles. 'We're 'avin' a sing-a-long, babes. But these fuckers – ' she jerks a thumb at the pretty one and the beautiful one – 'won't let him play no Oasis.'

He puts his hands on his hips, bike clamped between thighs, and looks down at the pretty one and the beautiful one. 'What's the story, morning glory?'

'Oh, fuck off with your morning glory,' says the pretty one.

'If you are mean to me I shall not invite you to my party.'

'What party?'

'Ah!' He flashes a dark, theatrical smile. 'Now that would be telling.'

'Oh, here he goes,' says the homeless woman.

He gets back on his bike and starts to ride in little circles in front of the museum steps. 'I am but a simple messenger boy! I come gathering the wild and the deranged. Come to my party!' He does a wheelie and spins around, coming to a stop.

'Where's it to?' says the homeless woman.

'Follow and I shall show you.' He beckons us with a wave of his arm. 'Come one, come all!'

The homeless woman gets up. 'Oh, all right. If we ain't gettin' any Oasis, I ain't stickin' around here.' She pulls her trousers out from between her buttocks and looks down at us. 'Are yow lot comin'?'

The pretty girl looks at her beautiful friend then back to the homeless woman. 'Do you know where it is?'

She shakes her head. 'Let the bastid have his fun.'

'Follow, follow, follow me!' calls the man, riding around in figures of eight now.

'I reckon we should,' says the beautiful one to her friend.

'Ooh, the mystery,' says her friend. 'The adventure.'

'The intrigue,' says the beautiful one.

They stand up, grabbing their tobacco and bags off the floor. Not me. Not in a million years.

'Come one, come all!' calls the man on the bike.

'Oh, shut yer fuckin' face, we're comin',' says the homeless woman. 'This better be a good party now. I want me jollies.'

They all start walking after the man on the bike, except for the guitar player, who stays sat on the steps.

The beautiful one turns back.

'Come on then, Blondie.'

She smiles with those soft, soft lips.

Her name is Isobel. When she tells me this my hands go cold. Because of the Björk song. It means nothing, I tell myself. That was ages ago. That was silly. A year-old delusion. Means nothing. Not if you don't indulge it.

I ask her friend, the pretty red-haired one, what her name is.

If it's Peggy, I'm going to run. I'm going to run until my legs collapse.

'Siân,' she says. 'What was yours again?'

'Sylvester.'

The man on the bike is up ahead, cycling in slow circles. It's dark. The street lights are still on. I think of the moonlight on my dad's grass. His slouched back. Aled Mellor's poor white pants.

Seroxat, Seraquin, Seroquel, aspirin. *Asssperin*. Asperoni. Esperanti. Timolol.

'This is mad,' says Isobel. 'He could be leading us anywhere.'

'Probably a squat party full of crusties,' says Siân. She looks at me. 'What do you think about all this, Sebastian?'

Isobel elbows her. 'His name's Sylvester! Don't be rude.'

'You fancy him,' says Siân.

I stare at the road ahead, my neck hot. I imagine her holding my hand, me holding back, nervelessly, even stroking her knuckle with my finger the way some couples do, just stroking it, mindlessly, in little circles which adhere to no pattern; her lying across my lap while we watch *Terminator*, me stroking her hair. Her spread-eagled face down on my bed with her cheeks spread wide. My dad aiming his ejaculate onto her brown-tinged anus.

Timolol, alfacalcidol, chloramphenicol, tramadol, timolol, tramadol, timolol. Blessed timolol.

It's been half an hour now and we're still walking, and the Pied Biker, as I've chosen to call him, in my mind, because it's not funny enough to say out loud, he's still telling us to follow, follow, follow, weaving around us in lazy figures of eight, sometimes seeming to disappear into the darkness for a few minutes, making us wonder aloud if this is all some kind of prank, that he'll go and stay gone, and we'll be left in the middle of Pontcanna, standing like lost cattle in the middle of the silent road.

'He'd do it 'n'all,' says the homeless woman, who I now know is called Gypsy, and who is not homeless after all, so I was wrong to judge from appearances. Gypsy's an ex-art teacher who got sacked for coming to class drunk, and now she lives with her younger boyfriend in Splott, and she claims disability for a bad back, which is not a scam, because though she is mostly fine, at least twice a year her back goes and she's stuck lying in bed for a week, medicated with buprenorphine and urinating into a jug.

'We have arrived at our destination!' calls the Pied Biker. 'Please do not disengage your seat belts until we are safely landed!'

He's stood at the end of the street, bike wedged between his thighs. He does a theatrical bow, fluttering his hands in circles. He's outside a large terraced house. There's a balloon tied up to the front railing.

A red balloon.

My stomach turns into a black hole.

'Is this a squat party?' asks Siân.

'It's a little gathering of friends,' says the Pied Biker.

I stop. Breathe. If I walk in there, Björk will be playing. Or Peggy Lee. Probably Björk. This is it.

'You coming or what, Blondie,' says Isobel. Isobel. Why did I ignore the signs? They were slapped in the palm of my hand like a pumping black heart.

She takes my hand and I get that same feeling I get whenever Patty touches me – an electric mixture of warmth and pleasure and desire and fear and discomfort and revulsion – but this time more violent, and I follow her in, like a little boy following his mother into an old lady's strange-smelling flat.

Björk is not playing. 'Hey Ya' by Outkast is playing. And you can't make 'Hey Ya' mean anything.

'What the fuck's this?' says Gypsy. 'I thought yow were bringin' us to a house party.'

'Ah,' says the Pied Biker, holding up a finger, 'but it will be. All parties have their beginnings and this is the beginning.'

'I've got blisters from that walk, I have.'

'Then come and rest your weary feet, my lamb.'

Siân and Isobel are looking around with cyanide in their eyes. It's a big empty house with no furniture, just a couple of sleeping bags of various colours kicked up against the walls, colours which mean nothing. The lighting is provided by lots of big, melty candles. As well as us, the newcomers, there are five people sat around on the floor, smoking in silence.

'Squat full of crusties,' whispers Siân to Isobel.

'Yow got any funsies?' says Gypsy to the Pied Biker, leaning against a wall, drinking from her can. 'I ain't got no money but I can give yow a lap dance.'

They all laugh at this. Not me. Isobel's palm is hot and sweaty. What am I doing here? In this house of strangers with a red balloon outside, red for danger, and a man in a back garden across town with his poor white underpants showing.

Her hand feels disgusting.

Isobel doesn't eat any of the mushrooms. They're muddy. She looks at them with squirmy-mouthed disdain. If I ate those, my mind would go. It'd be like getting a plunger and unblocking a kitchen sink and all the years of fat and rotten vegetables and slimy pasta chunks coming up in a gurgling burp.

I honestly think it would kill me.

Siân eats a handful of them, grimacing. 'Foul little fuckers, aren't they?' Gypsy has some too, but she doesn't seem to mind the taste. She rolls them up into squidgy black balls and washes them down like tablets with her Special Brew.

'Hey Ya' finishes. There's a pause. And then it starts again. This is the third time.

We're sat away from the other people. They're silent. There's four men and a woman. They all have nose piercings. Just one nose piercing each, no others, small silver rings glimmering in the candle light. Like they're in some sort of gang. Or sect.

Isobel's hand is on my knee. Plonked there all heavy and hot like a cooked mackerel. I can feel a strange energy coming out of it. But my penis is responding, feeding off the strange energy, and my muscles are stiff too, my tendons, my trapezius. I imagine peeling her fingers off my knee. Re-directing them onto my crotch, where they pull the zipper down, slithering like worms

116

into the gap. Her fingertip sliding around the end of my penis in small circles. Around and around, spiralling out of the edges, a pattern, a snail shell. Then her finger dipping into my urethra, plunging all the way down to the knucklebone.

'Can I tell you a story?' I say to her. 'I'm good at telling stories.'

She smiles, cigarette smoke oozing out of her nostrils. 'Of course.'

'OK. So, there was this boy who had emerald-green eyes and white-blond hair, and the thing with this boy is, he had fourteen fathers, which is impossible, right? Except it wasn't impossible. Because a witch, a beautiful and cruel witch who had an understanding of magic and science, she had cast a spell on the DNA of fourteen men and made it so. And she did this because she was bored. Just bored. Because she had a massive intellect and she wasn't getting enough stimulation, and first she tried to solve this boredom with alcohol and drugs, but it just made her sick, and then she tried to solve it with religion, but she was too clever for religion. And then she tried to solve it by eating, and she got really fat, so fat that she couldn't walk anymore and had to have her apprentice witches wash her and help her to go to the toilet, and she got so fed up with the look on their faces as they scrubbed the moss from her armpits that she decided food was a terrible thing to fill a hole with, almost as bad as alcohol, so she stopped eating so much and did a spell to remove all the excess weight and all the cholesterol from her arteries, and the funny thing about the world this witch lives in, cholesterol isn't called cholesterol, it's called alfacalcidol, and it's bright green, like the boy's eyes. So anyway, she lost all the weight and decided she would solve her boredom with magic and invention, and that's how she ended up making a boy out of fourteen fathers.'

They're all looking at me.

'Wow,' says Siân, mouth hung open. 'That was amazing.'

'Did you just think that up just now?' says Isobel.

I nod.

'Yow are gonna mess with me head when these shrooms start workin',' says Gypsy.

'No, it'll be a*maz*ing,' says Siân. 'Will you tell me stories like that all night?'

'No, he's mine,' says Isobel, pressing my knee.

'Aw, look at the poor little fucker,' says Gypsy. 'Lamb to the slaughter.'

'Hey Ya' plays on. For the sixth time.

Fourteen times and I'm out of here.

'What is their fascination with this fucking song?' says Siân. 'It's creeping me out. It's doing my actual head in.'

The nose-ring gang sit quietly at their end of the room. They're not looking at us. The Pied Biker has been away for some time.

'I'm getting bad energy from this party,' says Siân. She leans forward to whisper, her pale cleavage squishing together: 'Imagine that guy on the bike led us here so he could kill us. And they're' – she cocks a thumb at the people on the other side of the room – 'in on it.' Siân's pupils are as big as squashed woodlice.

'Don't yow start spinnin' me out with yer paranoia, missy,' says Gypsy. 'First him with his stories, now yow with yer paranoia. Yow lot are a bunch of headfucks.'

'Imagine,' continues Siân, 'that guy on the bike is in the kitchen right now, holding a massive carving knife in his hand and just waiting for the right time. Like, a signal. A signal from *them*.'

'Please don't say things like that,' I say.

'Hey Ya' finishes. A moment's pause like dew about to drop. 'Hey Ya' starts again.

'Right, that's it,' says Gypsy, hoisting herself to her feet. 'Yow're all bumming me out. I'm going over to them murderers for a change of topic.' She stumbles to the other end of the room.

'Good,' says Isobel, once she's out of earshot, 'you can bum fags off them instead.'

'I honestly have a bad feeling about this place,' says Siân. She lets out a hysterical laugh. 'Literally.'

'Oh, here we go,' says Isobel, rolling her eyes. 'This is going to be a fun few hours.'

And her hand creeps up my thigh a little.

'Carry on with your story, Sebastian,' says Siân.

'Sylvester,' says Isobel.

'Whatever,' says Siân. 'Tell us another story, Sylvanian Families.'

'OK.' I shift around on my buttocks. 'So the boy has fourteen fathers, and they're all very different kinds of men. Shall I tell you about them?'

'Yes,' says Siân, eyes filled with awe.

'OK. So there was Joshua, who was an average sort, not very interesting, except he was very good at sex, and he might have made a good porn star but he would never do a thing like that because he knew it would bring shame on his mother, so he only applied his talent at leisure, and he had loads of girlfriends, and his speciality was cunnilingus.'

'Ooh, I love it,' says Siân.

Isobel's grip on my thigh tightens, just a little.

'*Then* there was Ian, who was a Catholic priest, only he wasn't one of those bad ones who hurt children, and even though he saw prostitutes quite regularly and he was very dirty, he was always nice to the prostitutes and he blessed them all the time, even though deep down he didn't believe in God, because his mother died when he was very young, and this had made him very disillusioned, but he became a priest anyway, because his mother had always wanted that for him. And then there was Peter, who, um … let me think. OK. Who was a *taxi driver*, yes, a taxi driver, and the interesting thing about him was, he had a fetish for cotton wool. But that's the only interesting thing about him. And then there were Andy and Randy, and these were identical twins, and they were clowns who did children's parties, making balloon animals and stuff, and the balloons were always red, red for danger, because Andy was a paedophile and he did horrible secret things at some of these parties, and his brother didn't know about it, and so far, he had got away with it, and the witch who did the spell on the fourteen men, she saw the wickedness in his DNA, and she found a way to punish him, but that's a whole other story.'

'Tell us,' says Isobel, her dead mackerel creeping up my thigh.

'OK. So, she locked up Andy in her dungeon and she had her apprentice warlocks go in and rape him every afternoon at two o'clock, which is fourteen o'clock, and she chose the warlocks with the biggest penises – in fact, she did a spell on them to make them even bigger, fourteen inches. So all of them had fourteen inch penises now, which they were grateful for, and because of the witch's clever magic, none of these men had to worry about erectile dysfunction, which often affects men with extra-large penises, so it was a win-win situation, although it meant that some women wouldn't have sex with them, because fourteen inches is a lot to accommodate, so maybe it wasn't a total win-win, but anyway, that's not important right now. So they each raped Andy every day at two o'clock, one after the other, and they didn't mind doing it because Andy was a paedophile and the witch had told them exactly what she'd seen in his DNA, and there were fourteen of them, these warlocks, so you can imagine, a lot of damage was done to Andy, especially since this went on for a month, and without lubrication. And at the end of the month, the witch looked into Andy's soul and saw that he wasn't changed, and that if she let him go, he'd carry on hurting children, so she sucked out his soul and trapped it inside a red balloon. And she kept the balloon tied to her bedpost and every night before going to sleep she asked him in a sarcastic way if he was enjoying himself, and smiled wickedly when his soul pressed against the balloon begging for release, and then she'd turn over and go to bed, and that's how she punished Andy.'

'Wow,' says Siân, staring at my face. 'You're like an oracle or something. Is that the right word? Oracle?' She smiles. 'Oracle. Oracle. That's a good word. Oracle.'

Isobel pushes her hand a little farther up my thigh. She leans over and whispers in my ear, 'I want to fuck you.'

'What did you just say to him?' says Siân, looking worried.

'Nothing.'

I imagine Isobel on her hands and knees, backside in the air, vagina visible out the back like two peach segments. Anus slightly open. I imagine Siân licking hungrily, tongue going up, deep, then pulling out and going round the anus in circles, circles which adhere to no pattern. Then biting into the anus like it's a watermelon, biting and ripping.

'Hey Ya' finishes. A pause. Starts again.

'Can I carry on with my story?'

They nod.

'OK. Um. Where was I?'

'The paedophile. Andy.'

'Yeah, yeah. OK.' I take in a long suck of air through too-dry lips. 'OK. So. That was Andy and his twin brother Sandy – no, Randy. Like I said, Randy didn't know about his brother being a child molester, and he was mostly a nice man, although he was secretly claiming DLA, even though there was nothing wrong with him. And then there was Naveed, who was a Muslim, a very devout Muslim who prayed on his prayer rug all the time, and he was fat, like properly fat, and he blamed it on his metabolism, but really it was because he ate too much and never exercised, but his wife fancied fat men so it wasn't so bad. Anyway. Mostly, Naveed was a nice man, except he was sexist. And all he wanted was a son, but he'd only had daughters and his wife was too old to have more children, so this is why he agreed to take part in the witch's magical experiment, because it would mean he would have one fourteenth of a son, and that was better than nothing. And the witch, she could see this sexism in his heart, and at first she was angry, because she was a militant feminist, but when she looked deeper she saw that this sexism was a product of his culture and religion, so it wasn't really his fault. But all the same, she couldn't let it slide completely, because she was a vindictive witch, and also she read the *Daily Mail*, which she thought she enjoyed in an ironic way, but this wasn't really true, and she was in fact a bit racist and deep down thought all Muslims were terrible. So anyway, she decided to make an example out of Naveed. Do you want to know how she did this?'

'Yes,' they say in unison. Isobel has taken her hand off my leg so she can roll a cigarette.

'Well. It was simple. She used her science and magic to turn Naveed's youngest daughter into a transsexual. Sorry – a *transgendered* person.'

'Oh, wow,' says Siân.

I nod. 'This daughter was called Asha, and until the witch did her curse she was a normal girl who liked to play with dolls and things like that. But once the curse was done, Asha's personality changed. She became a tomboy and threw all her dolls away, and she grew up feeling like a boy inside, and because she was a Muslim living in a Muslim community, this was very hard for her, but in sixth-form college she made friends with some gay people who were involved with political activism and things like that, and they became like family to her and gave her the courage to undergo a sex change on the NHS, even though it meant shaming her real family, but she did it anyway because being a woman made her self-harm with razor blades. So anyway. She started taking hormones and grew a beard and she had all the operations and changed her name to – um, let's see…'

'Manfanny,' says Siân, grinning.

'No,' I say, a bit crossly. 'Sudeep. She changed her name to Sudeep. And the Muslim community rejected her, sorry – *him*, and Naveed was shamed forever, and in the mosque all the Muslim priests – imams, I think they're called – they acted like he'd done something wrong and they said things like, "If you cannot control your daughter, you are weak in the eyes of Allah," which isn't very nice, and to add insult to injury, Sudeep travelled to America to go on *The Oprah Winfrey Show* to talk about his experience – does Oprah Winfrey still have a chat show?'

They both shrug.

'Well, in this story she does. And anyway, she went on the show – sorry, *he* went on the show – and the wicked witch was in the audience, laughing, because she'd had her revenge on the sexist man who wanted a son. And when Sudeep started telling Oprah about the device he used to pump up his little penis, the witch broke down into a fit of laughter and started to hyperventilate, and Oprah got angry because this was a very serious subject matter, and she looked into the audience to find the laughing person, but by then the witch had vanished.'

I look at my audience.

'That's amazing,' says Siân, her eyes almost pulsating in her head. 'You should write this down.'

Isobel is licking her cigarette paper. I watch her. She knows I'm watching. She licks the paper extra slow then winks.

'I need a piss,' says Siân, frowning.

Isobel lights her cigarette. 'Go and piss then.'

'You've got to come with me. Seriously.'

'You can piss on your own, Siân. *Seriously.*'

Siân grabs Isobel's arm. 'Please, don't be mean.' She looks at me. 'Oracle, tell her to come with me.'

'Maybe you should go with her,' I say, because if she doesn't then it's just me and Isobel with her dead mackerel.

'We'll both come with you,' says Isobel, breathing out smoke. 'We'll stand outside and keep watch.' She stands up in a clumsy way, her legs going askew, and I can see up her dress. Of course – red knickers.

'Timolol, latanoprost, timolol, timolol.'

'What?' says Isobel, helping Siân to her feet.

I realise I've said it out loud. 'Nothing. Just words.'

'You're a strange little bunny,' says Isobel, kissing me on the mouth. It's quick and warm and wet. I smile stupidly.

Isobel yells across the room, asking where the toilet is, and one of the nose-ring gang tell her it's just across the hall in a deadpan voice.

'Hey Ya' is still playing.

Siân casts her eyes around the room, at the candles and the blank white walls. She focuses on the sleeping bags rucked up against the wall. 'Are there people in those?'

'No,' says Isobel.

'Are you sure?' She takes a big breath in through her nose. 'I think there are. I think they're hiding.' She grimaces.

Isobel takes her hand. 'Come on, let's get you to the toilet.' And she takes my hand too, her in the middle, and we walk together to the door. 'Your hands are ice-cold,' she tells me, and I nod.

Once the toilet door is shut, Isobel is on me. Kissing me, rubbing up against me, grabbing my hair. Her spit is like ashtrays and beer. Her lips are hard, her tongue both spongy and stabbing.

'Isobel!'

She yanks her mouth away from mine and shouts 'What!?' at the door.

'Can you come in a minute?' says Siân. 'Just a minute? Please?'

'Fucksake, Siân.' She has a scrunched little face and vinegar dribbling out of her eyes. 'One sec.' She goes in the toilet.

'Hey, hey.'

I spin around. It's the Pied Biker, coming down the stairs. He's only wearing trousers now, his torso bare. He's corpse-pale and hairless and he's got a bluebottle tattooed on the centre of his chest. He comes down slowly, one hand on the banister. He's under a bare light bulb, half his face in shadow, and for a second the shadowy bits seem to seep and form around his eye sockets and cheekbones and I see a face, a face on top of his face, like a

124

mask. It's sarcastic and sinister and reminds me of one of the thirteen faces, but it's not, so maybe it's the fourteenth face, finally, and it's followed me all the way from Dad's flat to this large empty house in Pontcanna, and the fly has come back too.

'Hey, where you going, fella?' says the Pied Biker.

'I need to go home,' I say, scrabbling with the front door lock as 'Hey Ya' finishes once more – a pause – and starts once more. My back is crawling. Like there's a sheet of glass splinters held up behind me by a telekinetic mind, and any minute it'll all slam into my back, puncturing my lungs, so that I freeze with blood dribbling out of my mouth then drop down dead.

'Thanks for coming, tell your friends!' he calls, as I open the door and run outside, down the path, past the red balloon.

Which.

Means.

Nothing.

The Fourteen Fathers

You should never look back when you're scared of illogical things. You should breathe deep and walk slow. Looking back only makes it worse.

The streets are totally empty. Just lines and lines of parked cars. It's not a good thing, being so alone like this. You can hear your own footsteps. Your own breath. It's not good to listen to your own footsteps and breath when you're scared.

This one time I was walking home from Patty's and it was four in the morning and the streets were empty, like this. Allensbank Road, it was, which is a very long, car-lined street with nice houses and big trees, and on one end, a cemetery. But it wasn't the cemetery that gave me the problem, not at first. It was the cars. The endless rows of vacant cars. I started imagining there were body bags in all the cars. Slumped upright in the seats. With dead people inside. And because it was so dark, my eyes started playing tricks on me, which is a cruel thing for the eyes to do. I'd see dark shapes in the cars up ahead. The headrests of the seats. But through the rear windows they looked like the tops of body bags. And I started to imagine the dead bodies waking up. The thick rubber of the bag creaking. Twisting. And at one point I even heard the sound of a zipper coming undone. My ears playing tricks on me. Teaming up with the eyes. And so I panicked and started sprinting. Like I said, it's a long road, and very straight. I was fit enough to manage the running, but I didn't think that my heart could take the fear. Sometimes that happens – you feel like the panic is so big, it could push you into cardiac arrest. So I ran and I ran and I ran, looking back, looking left and right, heart booming, and then I got to Cathays Cemetery. And I couldn't deal with it. No way, not with my mum in there. So I turned down Llanishen Street, even though it would take me ages out of the way, and this was another car-lined silent street, with an old school on one side, one built at the turn of the century, and it wasn't as bad as a cemetery, but it was still bad. Ghost children in little raggy uniforms and peaked caps, rasping words at me through tiny teeth. Soon I was on Whitchurch Road, which has lots of shops. I caught my breath then walked the rest of the way home, glad of the slowly approaching men for a change, not even crossing the street.

And this is why no people can be just as bad as people. You can't win sometimes.

I should get a taxi somewhere. Patty's maybe. My mind is crawling like a deep grave. If I'm seeing faces on top of faces then I should get a taxi.

The driver leaves me alone. Because my eyes are closed. If only you could do that all the time – close your eyes and the world leaves you alone.

Patty lives next door to a Malaysian restaurant. Which is better than living next door to a dead man.

Her flat is small and messy, but it's not a horrible kind of mess. It's an arty kind of mess. She has leopard print everywhere – throws and cushions and rugs, and lots of pink things, even though she's fundamentally against girls liking pink, and plans to dress her future daughters in androgynous colours. She also has lots of pictures of topless burlesque women on her walls, even though she's against the objectifying of women. Her argument is that it's OK for other women to look at pictures of nude women, because women don't objectify, they appreciate. I asked her once if it's OK for men to appreciate pictures of nude women, so long as they don't objectify them, and she said, 'Sure.' And then I asked her if it was OK for women to objectify men, and she said, 'Sure.' Because, she claimed, women are the subjugated and men are the subjugators, so it's fine, in the same way as it's fine for black comedians to make fun of white people, but it's not OK the other way around.

And so we went back to making our mix CD together, and when we were finished we decided to call it *The Subjugated and the Subjugators*. Then I went home and looked up 'subjugation' in the dictionary. And it meant what I thought it'd meant.

It must be around five in the morning when the taxi pulls up outside her flat. I expect a red balloon tied up to her gate, bobbing ominously like a dead hand in a river, but of course this is stupid, and there is no red balloon. I pay the taxi driver. It's still dark but the birdsong is getting louder.

It's too early to wake Patty up, so I decide I'll just sit on her front step until it's OK to knock. I could tell myself stories. Or maybe, I think, I could stop running away from my thoughts and confront the issue of the possibly dead man. Because this isn't just some paranoid thing inside my brain; it's a real-life thing. I'm not a little boy. You will deal with this, Sylvester Skillacorn, I tell myself. It's a real-life thing. You will deal with it.

Now what are you going to *do*?

So. There was the Muslim father, Naveed. And then there was Jimmy Joe, and he was a biker. He was born in Pontypridd, and then, when he was ten, his family moved to Scotland. And they all died from natural causes, except it didn't seem natural, because they all died in the same week, his mother and father and brothers and sisters and even his grandparents, all of them died from things like cancer and heart problems and brain problems, all in the same week, so even though it was natural, it was also a freak thing, and they might as well have died in a car crash or something. But what Jimmy Joe didn't know was that the witch was behind it. See, this was when she was going through her drugs and alcohol phase, and she was drinking Jack Daniel's all day, just like Janis Joplin, and she was also taking heroin and cocaine and LSD and crystal meth, and by the way, it was her who invented crystal meth, because she was so good with science, and anyway, she was out of her mind on all the drugs and did lots of spells that she wouldn't normally do, and one of these was killing Jimmy Joe's family by giving them terminal cancer and heart defects, and she did this because she was hallucinating all the time, because of the drugs, and she'd hallucinated that Jimmy Joe's family were devil people with twisting black faces and twisting black souls, and when she came out of her hallucination and saw what she'd done, she felt terrible, and realised she'd hit rock-bottom. And that was when she stopped taking drugs. And she felt so guilty about what she'd done to Jimmy Joe's family that she approached him about taking part in her experiment, thinking that it would make him feel better, helping to create a son, but she knew that this wasn't enough, so she also decided that she would bless him with good fortune, and after that he won the lottery and fell in love with a woman who was beautiful and intelligent and brilliant in bed, and very funny, and kind to people and animals, and one hundred per cent loyal, but not a doormat or anything, so he still respected her, and they got married on a beach with flowers in their hair and they had four children together and lived a blessed life and the witch didn't feel so bad any more. But that was in Jimmy Joe's future. Right now he was taking part in the witch's experiment and was very lonely and sad and drank lots of beer, and he was mostly a nice person, except he'd once raped a girl when he was sixteen, although it had been one of those rapes that was a bit grey, because the girl had said yes, yes, yes until the last minute, then said no, stop, just before he was ready to ejaculate, and he couldn't stop himself and ejaculated in her anyway, so it was still a rape and he felt bad about it, but it could have been worse, and the witch knew about it, but she kind of let it go, since she'd murdered his whole family.

And then there was Christine, who was a transsexual, but who still had a working penis and testicles. The witch had chosen Christine just because she thought it was funny, which is quite mean actually, because transsexuals shouldn't be laughed at or turned into novelty characters, but that was the witch all over. Anyway, Christine was born Christopher and Christopher got sent to prison for armed robbery, which he committed while high on crystal meth, which was invented by the witch, remember, and this was an American prison, because Christopher was American, and it was one of those awful American prisons like in the documentaries where all the white people hate the black people and vice versa and all the inmates turn their toothbrushes into knives, and there's lots of raping. And Christopher, he was a small and pretty man, so straight away he became an easy target for the rapists, and he decided that the only way to survive would be to belong to one of the gang leaders, for protection, so he tried to catch the eye of the hardest, most powerful man, who was a black man called Tiger Chunks, and he did this by doing some research and finding out that Tiger Chunks liked ladyboys, so he swapped his last packet of cigarettes for a cheap wig and started to act like a woman, and soon Tiger Chunks noticed him and pursued him, and Christopher became Tiger Chunk's woman, and from then on he was safe from all the other rapists. And he soon discovered that living as a woman felt good, and he was amazed that this was the case, because he'd always felt normal, not that there is such a thing as normal, and soon he swapped his cheap wig for a better one and the other prison transvestites showed him how to put on make-up, and he felt reborn and decided to go by the name Christine. And when she got out of prison seven years later, she carried on with the lifestyle and started to take hormones, which is a very expensive thing to do in America, because they don't have the NHS like we do, but she'd got a degree in business management when she was inside, so she started up her own wig-making business and made lots of money.

Anyway, she agreed to do the witch's experiment because she was due to have her genitals removed soon, and wanted the opportunity to have a child before it was too late, and she didn't mind that it would only be one-fourteenth of a child.

And the next father was Tiger Chunks, who we already know. He was in prison for life because he'd killed a bunch of people. As I've said, Tiger Chunks was the most powerful man in prison, and this is because he was fearless and very clever, and he understood power better than anyone else, and in another life, he probably would have made a good politician, but being a poor black man brought up in the Bronx, his life was pretty much laid out for him as soon as he was born, because black people in the Bronx have it pretty rough, and it's not like in Britain where lots of poor people get their tuition fees paid by the government, and in all honesty, I'm just glad I'm white and British, which is very selfish, I know. So anyway, he started out selling drugs on his bicycle at the age of six and he killed his first person when he was twelve, which is awful, and he was so clever that he became a big crime boss by the age of sixteen, and he killed all these people and got sent to prison, and he was thirty by the time he met Christine, or Christopher, as she was at the time, and he fell in love with her, even though he wasn't really gay underneath and probably would have been married to a real woman by now – sorry, a cis woman – if he wasn't in prison, but that's the thing about prison, it brings out a man's homosexuality, and even though he just started off by having men give him oral sex, after five years inside he was kissing them and even doing oral sex himself. But only the ones dressed as women. And by the way, he was called Tiger Chunks because, in his early gangster days, he had a really powerful gun, and when he killed people with it, he blew them into chunks. But Tiger was a nickname his mum had given him, because when he was a little baby he would scratch her when he was hungry, like a little tiger, and his real name was Marshall Mazey, which is actually a good name, so the nickname wasn't really necessary.

The Fly and the Dead Spider Ghosts

When the door swings open I'm reminded of the film *Misery* and the bits where Annie Wilkes goes into a three-day depression and looms over the writer's bed with dead old eyes and a face all turned down. Patty's wearing a leopard-print dressing gown, which makes her look a lot bigger than she is. Her face is shiny like a block of lard. Her lips are chapped and stained purply-black with wine. She hasn't got her eyebrows on.

'Sylvester?' Her voice is like rust.

'Hi, Patty. Sorry. I don't have anywhere else to go.'

She squints at me then clears her throat. 'OK. Well, come in.'

She lets me in and I follow her up the stairs. She's wearing big fluffy socks, red ones, which means nothing, and her calves are stubbly. I feel bad. Patty doesn't like people to see her in her natural state.

Her flat is messier than ever. It smells bad. The kind of smell your bedroom gets when you've had the flu for a couple of days. Cheesy. There are empty bottles of wine everywhere, and pizza boxes filled with old crusts and cigarette ends.

'Sorry it's so disgusting here,' she says, croakily. 'Make yourself at home, help yourself to whatever's in the fridge. I'm going back to bed.'

'Patty?' I say. 'Are you OK?'

She turns to me with slow shoulders. 'Not particularly.' Her eyes are so dead.

'Um. Do you want to talk about it?'

'I want to go back to bed.'

The only thing I can find to eat is some cornflakes. I eat them dry out of the box. The only good thing I can say about the cornflakes is they aren't completely stale. I drink some water from the tap, scooping it with my hands and slurping it up.

I move some pizza boxes off the settee and sit down.

I'm not going to be able to sleep. I'm so tired that I'm seeing things out of the corner of my eye. The ghosts of all the spiders I've ever stepped on.

Imagine it really is ghosts?

Not the ghosts of dead spiders, but the ghosts of dead people? And you see them because mental exhaustion is like a finger lifting the veil that separates the living from the dead.

Maybe I'm surrounded by ghosts right now, and they're just floating around, looking at me through their self-pitying white eyes.

Maybe Aled Mellor is here. Waiting.

'You let me die,' he's saying. 'I left you the red balloon and you ignored it. Was it worth it, that awful kiss? My wife is a widow now.'

But I'm not surrounded by ghosts. I'm not.

Aled Mellor probably just has concussion. He'll be in A&E right now, having a doctor look in his ear and check his blood pressure, the lucky thing. He'll be frowning and saying, 'It was my bloody neighbour. Carl Skillacorn. I knew he was trouble the first time I saw him. But I've got the last laugh, because now he's in a police cell, and he'll be there for a long time.'

That's probably what's happening.

But I don't know. You hear stories about how amazing the human body is, how some people survive falling off fifty-foot balconies or having an axe wedged in their brain. But on the other hand, you read a story where a person is knocked off a bicycle going slow and taps their head on the ground like a chocolate orange being tapped against a wooden table and they die straight away. So it's mixed messages.

Either way my dad is going to be in big trouble.

My mind is busy as an ant farm even when I'm healthy and rested. Without sleep, the ants break loose.

I look around slowly. The air feels charged. It isn't. Everything is normal right now. Except it isn't. I stare at a corner of the room. It doesn't look right. There's something wrong with it. The quality of the air. Charged. Swirly. There's an electric guitar propped up and a basket of laundry. But it doesn't look right.

'Show yourself,' I whisper.

The words feel ridiculous now they're out of my mouth. But I say them again. 'Show yourself, Aled. Let me see you.'

I hear a thud in the other room and it's like a firework going off in my shoes.

Just Patty. Moving in her bed. Getting up to urinate in a pint glass. She does that sometimes. Better than a Dr. Martens shoe.

'I know you're there, Aled.'

I stare at the corner. Focus hard.

'I'm sorry, Aled. Really.'

Just the guitar and the laundry basket. But it feels *wrong*. The skin on my arms comes out all bumpy. Psychosomatic, maybe.

'Maybe maybe maybe.'

Did I just say that out loud?

'Yes.'

I get this idea all of a sudden that if I went and picked up the guitar, Aled's spirit would guide my fingers and I would play spontaneous notes which would be the musical equivalent of his ghost voice.

'That's ridiculous.'

His spirit flowing through my hands, communicating his words along the fretboard, plucking at the strings. An arpeggio of dead despair.

'Ridiculous.'

And that would explain why the air seems so charged over in that corner.

'Stupid. Stupid.'

So I get up and I go to the guitar. Pick it up. It's cold and heavy. I take it back to the couch and sit down. I put my fingers on the frets, dangle my other hand over the strings. Wait.

Nothing.

'This is stupid.'

And then I think. In order for Aled Mellor's ghost to move my fingers and play his words, he'd have to know how to play the guitar himself. His alive self would need to have learned. And obviously he never did.

I move my fingers into A minor. Strum once. 'You're not really there. I'm just in a room on a couch, that's all. Talking to myself. Overtired. You're probably in the hospital right now. You're probably OK. I bet you have a concussion, and the doctors need to keep you in a while for supervision, but you'll be OK.'

'Who are you talking to?'

I drop the guitar. It flips as it falls and lands on my feet.

'Come in here and break all my stuff, why don't you?' says Patty. She's in the doorway, holding a bottle of red wine.

'Sorry,' I say. I pick up the guitar, prop it gently against the coffee table.

'Who were you talking to?'

'Just myself.'

'You said something about concussion.'

'Yeah. Just … rambling.'

She comes over and sits by me. 'I need a break from my bedroom. It's starting to smell.' She takes her tobacco pouch out of her dressing gown pocket and starts rolling a cigarette. 'I haven't had a shower in days. Or brushed my teeth.' She licks the licorice paper. I remember Isobel, her tongue dancing along the paper. 'So what brings you over?'

'I had to get away from my dad.'

'He being an arsehole again?'

'I guess so.'

She lights her cigarette. 'Call a spade a spade, Skillacorn. And an arsehole an arsehole.' She drinks some wine. 'You look awful.'

'I haven't slept.'

She nods. 'That'll be it. See, for me, it's the opposite. I've slept too much. That's why *I* look like shit.'

'Do you want to talk?' I say.

She shakes her head. Drinks more wine. Wipes her mouth. 'Breakfast of champions.' She looks at the bottle's label. '"Blackberry tones with eastern spices and a distinct oak smokiness." Bollocks.'

'What does it taste like?' I say.

'Blood and piss and vinegar.' She tilts the bottle my way. 'Wanna try some?'

I shake my head.

'Ever heard of Bukowski?' she says.

'Yes. But I've never read any of his stuff. Is it good?'

'I think so. But he's a sexist dick so I kind of feel I'm betraying the sisterhood, ya know? Well. I read in one of his books that every now and then he liked to stay in bed for three days. He liked to take his phone off the hook and stay in bed for three days, just drinking a few beers and vegetating, alone. He reckoned it was good for his soul. Like, he felt good as new by the end of the three days.' She sits back, the bottle of wine on her crotch. 'I've been trying it. I don't feel all that rejuvenated yet if I'm being honest.'

'It doesn't sound like a healthy thing to do,' I say.

'No,' she agrees. 'It's a fucking stupid thing to do.'

'I've been in my bedroom for three days too,' I say. 'Until last night. Only I wasn't drinking.'

'What were you doing?'

'Driving myself crazy.'

'Wanna talk about it?'

'No.'

She does a small, wry smile. 'Perhaps we should both just admit that we're fucking bonkers and go on the meds.'

'I don't want to go on medication.'

She shakes her head sadly. 'Me neither.' She tilts her head back, closing her eyes. She stays this way for a long while and I start thinking she's asleep, but then she suddenly snaps her head forward and drinks more wine. 'By the way,' she says. 'Last time I saw you – what happened there? I don't remember much. I have a vague memory of being in a park. Did I do anything awful?'

I shake my head. 'No. You were fine. You just drank too much and vomited.'

She looks at me closely. 'Are you sure? You're not just trying to spare me, are you?'

'No. You were fine.'

She nods. 'OK.' She looks at the slit of light coming through the curtains. 'I should try and go outside later. Get some sunshine. Serotonin and all that.'

'That'd probably help.'

She does a face shrug. 'I won't though. I know I won't.' She shifts around on the seat and lays her legs across my lap. 'Can I admit something really gross to you?'

I try not to look at her shins. 'OK.'

'Well. The last time I went on a bender like this I was on my period. And I was so miserable and drunk I didn't bother to change my tampon. And it got to the point where the tampon was so saturated it couldn't absorb any more. So all the blood just came out, and I didn't do anything about it.' She drinks more wine. Three long gulps. 'I just lay in bed letting my pyjamas and my sheets get all bloody. It stunk. And I started feeling so gross that I didn't care anymore. And I pissed the bed too. Deliberately. Just let it all come out.'

She looks at me with a bored sort of expectation.

'I had to throw the mattress away in the end.' She shifts around in the seat, her calves rubbing against my legs. 'Pretty foul, huh?'

'Yes.'

Patty smiles. She enjoys honesty. She finds it funny. 'I'm making you feel uncomfortable, aren't I?'

'Um, no. Not really. You've told me worse things.'

'Not that. My legs. Touching yours.'

'Oh, that. Yes.'

'Yes, it makes you uncomfortable?'

'Yes. You know it does.'

'But not as uncomfortable as, say, having your friend trying to suck you off in a children's play park?'

I look at her. 'I thought you couldn't remember.'

'I lied.' She smiles. 'And so did you.'

'I thought it would embarrass you.'

'It does. But I'm getting drunk now.' She tilts the wine bottle. 'Bottoms up and tally-ho.' And she drinks.

'I'm sorry,' I say.

'What for?'

'Lying.'

'No, it was nice of you.' The wine bottle is two-thirds empty.

'Was it that thing at the park that made you want to stay in bed for three days, Patty?'

'No. It wasn't really a big deal. Did I ever tell you about my mum's friend?'

I shake my head.

'Well, my mum had this friend, George. He was around fifty-something at the time. He's dead now. It must have been eight years ago, something like that, so I would've been fourteen. Yes, Sylvester, fourteen. An ominous number for you – I remember you telling me. Well, this one night, George comes round the house to see Mum, but Mum wasn't home. I can't remember where she was. Anyway, George invites himself in, says he'll wait for Mum. I say, "OK, but she might be out all night for all I know." But he doesn't mind. So he waits in the living room and helps himself to some beers. And because I've got nothing better to do, I join him. We watch TV and I have some beer too, even though I'm only fourteen. He doesn't care. He was this big hippy who smoked weed all day. He was nice actually. He had this really cool platonic thing going with Mum. Like, he was this really good friend to her, but he honestly didn't want to fuck her. And it's not like she was ugly or anything. Maybe they just weren't each other's type? Anyway. I had a bit of a thing for him. Probably because I was seeking a father figure, blah, blah, fucking blah. And after a while, I started to get drunk from all the beer. Being only fourteen and all that. So I decided to seduce him. Which was easy – all I had to do was put my hand on his dick. And in, like, minutes, he was fucking me on the couch. Taking my virginity actually. It was cool. Except I was all insecure because he was so old and experienced and I was so young and probably crap. So I felt like I had something to prove. And I was all, "Ooh, George, stick it in my arse." Thinking he'd be impressed, you know? Me, all dirty and worldly. Which was total bollocks – I actually had no great desire to be screwed up the arse. But I thought it would be cool. Sort of rock 'n' roll. So he does it – up my arse. And it's *horrible*. He used spit to lube me up, and even though he does it really slow, it fucking kills. Though I pretend it doesn't. And after a while he comes, and then he pulls it out, and when he does, this big load of shit comes out too. This big splurge, all over the sofa. Shit and cum. And I was so embarrassed I started to cry. And of course, this freaked him out. There I am, a minor, crying because I've just shat after anal sex. And he's got his arm around me, trying to console me, and there's the shit on the couch, seeping through into the cushion, and then, guess what I do?'

I shake my head.

She smiles. 'I puke all over his shirt. All. Over it. Loads. You know? So there's the shit and the puke, and who knows when Mum will come home? And I'm so embarrassed and drunk I run upstairs to my room and lock the door and pass out on my bed.'

She drinks her wine.

'What happened?'

'Nothing. He must've cleaned it all up before Mum got back. The next morning the couch was all wet and smelling like disinfectant. He'd flipped the cushion over too. Mum never found out.'

'Well, that's a good thing,' I say.

She nods. 'He stopped coming to the house. Mum thought he was avoiding her. She got really upset about it actually. I feel shit about that.' She lights a cigarette and inhales, looking at the curls of smoke. 'Anyway. He's dead now. Brain tumour.'

She smokes and drinks. I'm probably not meant to say anything. I look at the gap between the curtains. This room is like a sucking pit.

'Anyway,' she says, finally, grinding her cigarette butt out on a half-eaten pizza slice on the floor, 'that thing in the park was nothing. Don't worry about it, honestly.'

'OK.' Her legs are heavy on my lap. I'm too afraid to move. 'Patty? He probably knew what he was doing. That George. Coming over your house when your mum wasn't home. Letting you drink with him.'

She raises a lazy sardonic brow. 'I've no doubt. But what difference does it make?'

'I'm just saying. It wasn't your fault, what happened.'

'I know. It's just a shame that my mum had to suffer because of it.' She tries to blink her eyes dry. 'And that poor couch.' She laughs. 'Can I tell you something else?'

'If you want.'

'I should warn you, it's really dark. Not gross this time. Dark.'

'OK.'

'I've been thinking about it a lot lately. Been stuck in my bed, drinking and remembering stuff. Stuff you thought you'd completely forgotten about, you know?'

'I'm not going to like it, am I?'

141

'No.'

'Will you feel better about it if you tell me?'

'No. But I want to tell you anyway.'

She finishes her wine, pulls her legs off my lap and stands up a little wobbly. 'I'm going to crack open another bottle. And when I come back, I'm going to tell you something horrible about myself. And you're going to hate me.'

'No, I won't.'

'We'll see about that.' She goes to the kitchen for more wine, and it's just me and the charged air.

'When I was little I had this friend called Sarah Jane. She was this really fucked up little ginger girl. We were like best friends and worst enemies. I remember we once started pulling each other's hair in the playground, and it was agony, and neither of us would let go, we both just kept pulling harder and harder, you know? Both of us full of agony and rage. Horrible.' Patty starts picking away at the wine label with a dirty fingernail. 'The dinner-ladies had to break us up in the end. We both had chunks of each other's hair in our hands.' She smiles. 'Horrible, stubborn little bitches, both of us. And *she* had an excuse – she was really fucked up because she had this awful home life. Her stepdad used to beat her up, I think, stuff like that. Her mother was this horrible skinny alcoholic who used to show up at the school gates pissed as a fart, shouting her head off. And here's the worst part – her stepbrother used to molest her. He came into her room sometimes and did stuff to her fanny. That's how she said it. Did stuff to her fanny.'

She draws in her chin, burps. 'So. This one day, Sarah told me she'd decided she was going to kill herself. She told me and I was like, "Hell, yeah, do it." I got really excited about it.' She grabs her tobacco off the table and starts rolling a cigarette. 'We spent the next couple of days planning it. We talked about how she'd do it. I wanted her to run out on the road in front of a fast truck, or jump off a cliff or something like that. Something bloody and violent. But she didn't want it to hurt. She'd heard about this woman once who'd stuffed her pockets with rocks and jumped into a lake, so she decided to do that. She planned a date too – the following week, on a – well, I don't remember the day. It was going to be Roath Park Lake. She was going to sneak in at night. She was deadly serious, and so was I. I *genuinely* wanted her to do it.' She licks her cigarette paper. 'Then, the day before she was due to do it, she suddenly backed out. She was all, "I'm not sure it's such a good idea. Cuz what if there's no heaven or ghosts or anything and I just die and stay dead." And I was gutted. I was like, "No, do it. Honestly, there *is* a heaven, swear to God, my Mum told me so." Which is bollocks – my mum's agnostic. But I really wanted her to do it. So I kept on trying to persuade her. I nagged her and nagged her. I came up with all these arguments for it. But she didn't do it. The end.'

Patty looks at me. 'What do you think of that, Skillacorn?'

I just stare at my knees.

She blows smoke in my face. 'Told you it was dark.'

'Do you think she remembers any of it now? The girl?'

Patty shrugs. 'Dunno. I'd be surprised if she was still alive actually.' She picks a strand of tobacco off her tongue, looks at it, rubs it on her dressing gown. 'Do you think it makes me an evil person?'

'I don't know. You were young. Young people aren't very nice.'

'But what if that younger me is the real me? Like, I'm all grown-up and nice now, relatively, but deep down, that's who I really am.'

'Have you ever read that book, *Lord of the Flies*?' I ask. 'Or seen the film?'

'Yes,' she says. 'Both.'

'Well. Those children did some pretty horrible things. Maybe that's just what children are like. Maybe you get more empathy as you get older.'

143

She blows smoke into her wine bottle and watches it creep out. 'Did you do anything like that when you were little? Anything cruel?'

I think about it. 'No,' I say.

'I didn't think so,' she says.

'Do you think you would do anything like that now?' I ask her.

She considers it, her cigarette hand frozen a few inches from her mouth. 'Not in a million years.'

'Well, then,' I say.

'I think I could be cruel to someone who was a total arsehole,' she says. 'But not someone vulnerable. Or maybe I could. Who knows?'

'If you don't know, maybe you should stop thinking about it,' I say. And it's a ridiculous thing to say, coming from me. It's what my dad would say. But never mind my dad.

She leans forward and burps. Stands up. Puts the bottle of wine on the coffee table. 'I'll leave you with that, my dearest darling.'

'Patty?' I say.

'Hm?'

'Why did you used to have a shower every time you saw an ice cream van?'

She smiles wryly. 'You think I was abused by an ice cream van man or something, don't you?'

'Maybe. Something like that. I don't know.'

'I honestly have no idea why I used to do that,' she says. 'I can't remember. But I wasn't abused by an ice cream van man. I should be so lucky – imagine all the free ice cream?' She does her chesty, barking laugh, showing a purple-stained tongue. 'Try and get some sleep.' And she goes back to bed.

I feel really stupid looking at that guitar now. And something else: the tuners at the end of the guitar, the shiny metal tuners, six of them. Perfect liquid metal, unblemished. Better than a light switch. Better than the tuners on my acoustic guitar at home. They're daubed with glitter glue. These are sublime. Which is a word tailor-made for them – *subbliime*. Like double cream dribbling slowly from a spoon – no, not a spoon. From a clean fingertip. Perfect.

I think about what Patty said, us surrendering to medication. I don't trust the pharmaceutical industry, even if they do think up such poetic names for their drugs. Citalopram, sertraline, mirtazapine – they're meant to help with all kinds of stuff, including anxiety and OCD, but can they take that tingle out of my fingertips?

You know some of the things I've tried?

I once went through a phase of wearing thin gloves. The kind the man who polishes the white snooker ball on TV wears. But I would have to take them off all the time to use the toilet and wash my hands and take baths and masturbate and eat sandwiches. And people made fun of me, especially Dad.

I once tried to graze my fingertips with fine sandpaper, thinking that if my fingertips were rough, I wouldn't want to run them over surfaces. But sometimes I would sand too hard and my fingers would bleed.

I put plasters on the ends of all my fingers, even my thumbs. It never worked when I was little because I didn't want it to work, but as an adult I did. And it didn't. The plasters would get dirty and peel off really quickly, and again, there was the problem with washing my hands and eating things and masturbating. It was unhygienic. When I peeled the plasters off, I was left with the tacky residue, and this inspired my next idea – I coated my fingertips with glue. But of course, this was stupid.

So nothing worked. And then I realised that if I couldn't stop my fingertips, the touchers, then my alternative was to focus on the touched, and that's when I started putting glitter glue on all my switches and buttons, which was OK, even if it didn't deal with the real problem.

If only Dr Hunter was trained in CBT therapy. I would be a star pupil.

It must be around 10 a.m. when the ants start running loose. Because of the bluebottle.

I noticed it after Patty went back to bed. I don't know if it flew in through an open window or a vent, or if it's been in the room with me the whole time. Maybe it's been following me all night.

It's flying around, perching on pizza crusts, walking up the walls. At first I thought it was just a trick of the eye. Another dead spider ghost. But it's a real thing. And a logical thing. This room is smelly and full of rotting food.

You know what I've been thinking?

The fly is Aled Mellor.

Crouched on a pizza crust, rubbing his little stick arms together, looking at me.

This is what he's saying:

'You didn't do anything when you saw the red balloon. You didn't do anything when you saw the fly tattoo on that man. I couldn't have made it more obvious. And you ignored me. Too busy locking tongues with that dirty drunk girl. Isobel. Another sign you chose to ignore. And now I'm dead and my soul is locked inside this fly. And when you sleep I'm going to crawl inside your ear and dig into your brain and nibble away at your grey matter, and you will finally see the fourteenth face, and it will be more terrible than you ever imagined. Because you let me die.'

I close my eyes. Open them. The fly is still there. Like an oil spill.

So. There was Tiger Chunks. And before him there was the transsexual. The transgendered person, I mean. What was his name? Her name? Christian? Anyway, it doesn't matter. After Tiger Chunks there was, um, there was ... God, I don't know. Let's see. Um. OK. There was another black man. Yes, another black man. Called Roger. Because if you only have one black person then that's tokenism, and tokenism is bad. Anyway. There was Roger, and he was really posh and refined and educated and he had a tiny penis. Because he was not a black stereotype. And he was born in Oxford, and his parents had been the only black professors at Oxford University, and they'd been brilliant academics who'd published lots of groundbreaking papers on linguistics and stuff like that, and now Roger was also a professor at Oxford University, except he wasn't at all brilliant, and he'd only done so well because of nepotism and because he was upper class and also to fill the university's quota for minorities. Tokenepotism. There's a new word. Like an Egyptian pharaoh. Anyway, Roger wasn't a good professor, and he slept with all his female students, and remember, he had a tiny penis, so he wasn't very good at sleeping with his students, and he didn't do cunnilingus either, because he was scared of the idea, though this fear was disguised by revulsion, as it often is, according to Patty's books on feminism, and anyway, these students he slept with would feel unfulfilled after the sex, but they did at least get top marks for their homework, even if their homework was bad, so that's something, I guess. And even though Roger was bad at sex and bad at his job, he was good at lots of other things, such as drawing and painting, and it's a shame he was pushed into academia by his parents, because he might have made a wonderful artist, and in fact, he sometimes painted the students he slept with, and the paintings were amazing, and the students were flattered by these paintings, which is maybe why they didn't go around telling people about the dirty old professor and his tiny penis, that as well as the good marks, and also all these students were white and middle class with lots of white guilt, and they didn't want to get a black man into trouble in case everyone accused them of white privilege, or something like that. So no one ever found out about Roger having sex with his students, except the witch, because she knew everything, but she didn't care, because it was all consensual and both parties were getting something out of it. See, the witch viewed life as a series of transactions, she was very cynical like that, and maybe she was

147

right, but I don't know. Anyway, she decided one day to pose as a pretty blonde student at one of Roger's lectures, because that was one way in which Roger adhered to the stereotype – is adhere the right word? Well, who cares, it's my story. She posed as a pretty blonde woman, using magic, not a wig, she wasn't an amateur, and after the lecture she spoke to him and made it clear she was up for some sex, and Roger, being a stereotype, leapt at the chance, and they both went back to his big posh house, where he lived alone, except for his cats, he had lots of cats, and they went up to his bedroom to have sex, except the witch didn't want to have sex with him because she knew he wasn't good at it, she knew everything, remember, and instead she asked him to paint her, and he got all paranoid and asked how she knew he liked to paint, and she said, "Because I can see it in your eyes, you have artist's eyes," and this wasn't true at all, Roger had normal boring eyes, but he believed it because he wanted to believe it, so he took her up to his attic room where all his painting things were kept, and she took all her clothes off and spread her legs, because she wanted it to be an explicit painting and she was very proud of her vagina, and so he mixed up his paints and started painting her, and then the weirdest thing happened. He was painting her vagina, which was lovely, she was right to be proud of it, and then all these bluebottles started to fly out of it, hundreds of them, and he froze and blinked a few times, thinking it was a hallucination, but it wasn't a hallucination, it was really happening, and the witch laughed and said, "Keep painting, they won't hurt you." And so he kept painting, even though his hands were shaking, and the bluebottles were flying about the place and he asked her if he should paint the bluebottles, and she laughed again, and said, "You can try." And he said, "If I could paint them, it would be a really amazing painting, it would be unique." And she thought about it for a while, and said, "That's true actually." So she put a spell on the bluebottles and they all froze in mid-air, and he said, "OK, that's good, but it'd be even better if you could make them

148

do that while they're coming out of your vagina." Except he didn't say vagina, he used a dirty word for it. And the witch agreed with him once again, and she used her magic to unfreeze the flies, then she sucked them all back into her vagina, and then she got them to fly out again, and she froze them in the act of flying out, and it looked crazy, and Roger got to work and painted it all, and like I said, he was an amazing painter, and he captured everything, even the glossiness of the flies' oil-spill bodies, and the witch lit a cigarette and said, "You know, Roger, if you try to sell this painting to an art gallery, a lot of people are going to think you have a deep-seated fear of vaginas." Except she didn't say vaginas, she used the same word Roger used, beginning with "c". And Roger said, "Well, that's not true." And the witch said, "Yes, it is. I know everything." And Roger said, "In that case it must be very subconscious," and the witch said, "It always is, you moron." And Roger was shocked, because no woman had ever dared call him a moron, but he was also aroused, because deep down he craved a mean and dominant woman, and he got an erection, and he finished the painting in a rush, and he asked the witch to get rid of the flies, and she did, she unfroze them and they all flew onto the wall, and then Roger went over to the witch and had sex with her, and he was so aroused that he did a good job for once, and the witch didn't mind that his penis was small, because she used her magic to shrink her vagina hole to needle size, so there was plenty of friction, and though it was by no means the best sex she'd ever had, it was the best sex she'd had all week, and afterwards they both lay there smoking, satisfied. And the witch said to him, "For God's sake, Roger, quit your job and start painting for a living." And Roger closed his eyes for a second, just a second, to think about this, and when he opened them again, the witch was gone. But the flies weren't. They were still on the wall, hundreds of them, and they were crawling around to form words, and the words spelled out, "Thank you for your sperm. It was a pleasure doing business." And after Roger read this, the flies

149

all dropped dead and landed on the floor in a big black pile. Like mouse droppings. And Roger went to look at his painting, and it was an amazing painting, and he sold it to the national gallery, and he called it—'

And the fly, it's on my arm, my bare arm.

I flinch and it flies away. I stand up and start walking around the room.

It's Aled. It really is Aled.

I hear its buzzing, *his* buzzing. I trip over a small pink lamp and fall on the floor. I get up and start frantically searching the room. I don't know what I'll do with him once I find him.

I've already killed him once.

I trip over again, and this time I bang my knee. I lie curled up for a while, clutching my knee. My mouth freezes into the shape of a stretched out elastic band. And then the buzzing again. Over my head, to the left. I get up and look at the coffee table. Dirty mugs, overflowing ashtrays, DVDs out of their cases, spilled liquid. My dad would get nauseous if his coffee table ever got like this, but never mind my dad, who cares about my dad? The buzzing has stopped. I feel like hitting something. I want to cry. I see the bottle of wine Patty left behind. Mostly full. Shiraz. A lovely word. Shiraz.

I take the bottle and sit back down on the couch.

Fudge it. That's what my mum would say.

The very fact of alcohol's horrible taste is evidence enough that it should never be drunk. A yellow triangle. It's like alcohol is outright saying, 'I am bad. I am a poison. Go on, taste me. See?' But people ignore this, and it says, 'Why are you still drinking me? I thought I made things clear enough.' It's crazy that people go on drinking after that first taste.

Illogical.

I read the label on the back of the bottle. Fruity, smoky, berries. It's none of these things. It's nasty. That's the best word for it.

Nasty. But I drink anyway, gagging a bit. I want it to do the things it does to other people. I want to be calm and sleepy. I need to stop thinking. I pinch my nose shut and take a few swallows. Gag. Repeat.

It doesn't take long for my head to feel all fuzzy. I have a low tolerance, like a child. I lean back on the couch. My trapezius muscles feel looser. I drink. Nasty. I close my eyes. I don't feel sleepy yet. But it's nice to close my eyes. To look at the colours behind my lids. A womb-like red at first, pulsating, and then lots of goldy-green swirling patterns. Like a xylophone. No, that's the wrong word. Kaleidoscope. Kal-eye-duh-scope.

I open my eyes and take another nasty mouthful. I look at the bottle. Two-thirds empty already. The rim is a smooth perfect circle. I touch it. Cold, hard. I start running my finger along its edge, round and round. Oops-a-daisy, I think, giggling. Never mind, I think. Just my fingertip and the smooth round glass. Not just round and round – there's a pattern. Like a snail shell. A spiral, starting at the inner rim and ending at the outer rim, then back again. It has to be just so. Perfect. Because, if I get it right, the fly will disappear, Aled will disappear. My fingertip is both relaxed and highly focused. Like that game with the zigzag metal wire and the loop that must travel along it without touching, because if you touch it there's an electric buzz.

I see something from the corner of my eye. Not a dead spider ghost. The fly. On the armrest, inches from me.

I slap my hand down on it. Lift my hand, slowly. Squashed black thing.

'Got the sucker,' I whisper. I throw back my head and laugh, and it feels good.

It worked, the pattern. It made Aled disappear.

What I want right now is Patty. I wonder if she'd like it if I woke her up and had sex with her.

Fucked her.

151

I giggle.

I wouldn't kiss her – she hasn't brushed her teeth in three days. But I could fuck her.

I get up and knock her door. No answer. I knock again. No answer. I don't knock a third time. That would be rude. I sit back on the couch. I unzip and masturbate. Patty slowly inserting the heel of a red stiletto into her anus. I ejaculate onto my hand and then go and wash it in the kitchen sink. I feel bad about all the dishes in the sink.

Still. I'm having fun.

Patty has more wine in the cupboard. I'm sure she wouldn't mind me having a bottle. We're friends. Good friends. But just to be safe, I take out my dad's wallet and I place a twenty-pound note in the cupboard. I close the door. Then I open it again. I don't even like money. I don't even want his murderous drug money. I put the whole wad in the cupboard.

It'll be a nice surprise for her.

The wine is Rioja this time. I don't know how to pronounce it. Ree-yo-hah. That's how I want it. Apparently it's also part Tempranillo. That's easy. Temp-rah-nillow. Ree-yo-hah and Temp-rah-nillow. This wine is mixed race.

I giggle to myself, looking through Patty's cupboards for an appropriate cup, because I don't want to be stuck doing dangerous finger spirals around the bottle rim again, even if it does kill flies. I find a mug which is chipped at the rim in two places, and this is perfect, because my finger won't want anything to do with a chipped rim, and then I wonder why I've never thought of this before, and I don't slap my forehead, because that only happens in films, but I should do, because this is an amazing oversight on my behalf.

Some things are so obvious.

Goodbye, special beaker.

The bottle is one of those new screw-top bottles, which is lucky, because I wouldn't know how to get a cork out. I open it and quickly pour some wine into the mug. I try not to look at it.

Dog's anus, I think.

I don't know why I think that.

The mug is white with 'Wake up to milk' written in yellow balloon writing. I take a sip. Nasty. But I drink it down. And then I pour myself another.

It all gets fuzzy after that.

The Minotaur

The clouds are the colour of old socks. My legs are taking me somewhere. They know where. My brain half knows. It is in on the conspiracy, but it denies the conspiracy.

Passing people look at me. I smile. 'Drunk, drunk, drunk, drunk, drunk,' I say.

'Pissed as a fart,' I say.

'Pissed as a cunt,' I say.

A man outside a shop frowns at me. 'There are lots of things worse than swearing,' I tell him. 'Like murdering next-door neighbours.'

I walk on. Drunk in the street in the morning. Drunk in the street in the morning. That has a nice rhythm to it. Drunk in the street in the morning, tumty tum tum.

My muscles are all loose and floppy and my stomach feels like it's full of warmed-up jam. Best of all, I reckon I could have sex. I could fuck. I also think I could make love. I could do all the things you're supposed to do. Stroke the cheek, nuzzle the neck, sink flesh against flesh, relax into it, like two jellyfish splodging together. I could hold a hand without thinking too much about it. Spoon afterwards.

'I could spoon! Me! I could spoon while holding spoons!'

I laugh up into the sky.

I stop in a newsagents for something to eat. A sandwich. They mostly have boring sandwiches – cheese and pickle, ham and cheese. I don't like boring sandwiches. I like them experimental.

'Sexy,' I whisper to myself, in front of the refrigerator. 'Sexy sandwiches.'

I pick out a falafel and chutney roll, which is the sexiest thing they've got on offer, and a large bag of salt and vinegar McCoys, which I would usually avoid because of high fat and salt content, but right now I'm full of booze, so I'll eat what I like.

Booze. Such a silly word. Booooze.

When I get to the counter I remember how I left all my money in Patty's cupboard. I wonder if I should just run out of the shop with my food, run and run, fast as a squirrel. But I've still got change from the taxi driver in my pocket.

'Close one,' I say, handing a five-pound note to the cashier, who is a middle-aged woman with tiny grey eyes and colourless lips.

'I thought I didn't have any money,' I say, 'but I do. So it's OK.'

She gives me a small, tight smile. Then my change.

'I like your jumper,' I say. 'It's very red. And there's nothing wrong with the colour red. It means nothing.' I lean my elbows on the counter. 'Can I tell you a story? I'm good at telling stories.'

She looks around nervously.

'There was a shopkeeper and she sold a sandwich to a young blond boy with apple-green eyes, and he left the shop and ate the sandwich, and it was a nice sandwich, though not as sexy as he would have liked, and the shopkeeper went on to have a lovely day. The end.'

I spin around and walk to the door, almost falling into a display box full of limited edition Kit Kats.

Sometimes I think there's something wrong with my chi because of the way my body and my mind are always rebelling against each other. No union. No loyalty. My mind is the worst – it even

156

rebels against itself. It self-harms, but with thoughts instead of razor blades.

Right now, it's my legs rebelling. Taking me somewhere they shouldn't.

There's an elderly lady up ahead pulling a wheel-along trolley. She's probably in her eighties and she has dyed black hair in a short curly style. I really don't know why all old ladies have short curly hair. I catch up with her and walk by her side for a while. She doesn't even notice. She's got these really sunken bloodhound eyes. They look sore. They probably need some timolol.

'Hello,' I say.

She revolves her shaky old head slowly in my direction.

'My name's Sylvester Skillacorn.'

She stares in a bemused way up into my face. 'What?'

'My name's Sylvester Skillacorn and I won't harm a fly.' I do a loud donkey laugh. 'Except I did this morning. But it's the only time.'

She stops her trolley and looks at me with her face all hangy. 'I don't hear well, sorry.'

'That's OK. Crisp?'

She looks at the bag, her bloodhound eyes trying to focus. She smiles. 'Oh no, I can't eat those.'

'I just had a sandwich, but it was really dry,' I say. 'So I stuffed crisps into it. My mum used to make me crisp sandwiches. I love crisp sandwiches.'

She stares at me like I'm some newfangled object from a *Jetsons* future.

'Can I tell you a story?' I say.

'Pardon?'

'Can I tell you a story?'

The cautious bemusement multiplies a thousand-fold. 'I need to get to the chemist, love.'

'Of course. You need your timolol. Anyway, it was nice talking to you.'

And I carry on walking. Drunk in the street in the morning. Dum dum deedum dum dum.

'So. After whats-his-name, the black artist, there was another father.' I'm speaking out loud in a huge booming voice, like the Pied Biker. 'I don't even know how many fathers there've been so far, but that doesn't matter, I could go on forever, there could be fourteen *thousand* fathers. The next father was called Polly-Olly-doo-dah. No, that's stupid. Don't be stupid, Skillacorn. The next father was also black. Why the hell not? Why the fuck not?'

I slap a hand over my mouth. I feel like I'm going to be struck by lightning.

'Not in public, Skillacorn,' I whisper, looking around.

'His name was Percy. No, that's a silly name for a black man. His name was Jerome. Jerome St. Black. And he was a bodybuilder. He had muscles growing on *top* of muscles, which is crazy, and he took steroids, *loads* of steroids, and he was always angry. You see, he was obsessed with having a body like Arnold Schwarzenegger in his heyday, and every day he spent six hours pumping iron, and he took all the steroids and drank all the protein shakes, and every morning he ate twenty boiled eggs, yes, *twenty*, and at lunch he ate five whole chickens, and at suppertime he ate ten whole salmon, and the only carbohydrates he allowed himself were carrots, and sometimes a bit of sweet potato, because sweet potato has a low GI, and his whole life was this – eating protein and lifting weights – and the reason for this is because he was bullied in school for being small and weak, which is very sad but also very predictable.'

I stop at some traffic lights. I don't press the button. I never press the button. Luckily there is another old woman, and she presses the button. This one isn't as old as the other one, and she doesn't have a wheel-along trolley, but she does have a short perm.

'Why is your hair short?' I ask her.

She pretends not to hear.

'And *anyway*, there isn't anything else to say about Percy, except

158

he was secretly in love with his auntie, and always had been. And also, his name wasn't Percy, it was Jerome.'

I burst out laughing.

The old lady looks straight ahead at the traffic.

'And the next father was ... um, let's see. The next father was *Carl*. Yes. Why not? Carl Skillacorn.'

The little green man comes up. I walk across the road. I'm not far now.

'Carl was a very complex human being, except he wasn't a proper human being. He was a minotaur, which is half-bull and half-man. And it was the witch, the awful witch who made him this way, using her magic and science. And she did this during her drugs phase, remember that? Just because she thought it would be funny to see how a minotaur would live in modern society. Minotaur being a metaphor for masculinity, obviously. But the witch didn't realise this because she was on lots of drugs. So it was subconscious. As things often are.'

I turn at Fairfax Road.

'So she turned Carl into a minotaur and watched him through her crystal ball, except it wasn't a crystal ball, because that's a cliché, it was a special plasma screen which she invented with her magic and science. So she watched his life through her special plasma screen, and she smoked lots of crack cocaine, which she invented remember, no, wait – it was crystal meth she invented – anyway, it doesn't matter, she smoked crystal meth and she laughed cruelly down her long beautiful nose as Carl destroyed everything in his life, including himself and his wife. Except that isn't fair. No, that isn't fair at all.' I bump my hip into a lamp post. 'It was cancer that destroyed his wife, just mean old cancer, and Carl had nothing to do with that, nor the witch, it just happened, and it was very sad for Carl, because he loved her, even though she'd left him, wanting a separation, a few months earlier, he still loved her, so it was very sad, but you shouldn't feel too sorry for him, because after she died he was like a bull in a china shop—'

159

I burst out laughing and a man across the street with his hands in his pockets glances over mistrustfully – 'and he was mean to everyone, and once he even broke his son's nose, and his son was a fragile little thing with emerald-green eyes and white-blond hair, in fact, he was made of exquisite porcelain, which was also the work of the witch – see how imaginative she could be? *Awful*, just awful. And anyway, his nose got broken by the minotaur and it exploded into a million shards of fine glass and it all sprinkled onto the carpet like snowflakes, but luckily, nothing else got broke, but he was so upset that he moved out of the minotaur's labyrinth and lived for a year in a small house in Llandaff North. But you shouldn't feel too sorry for this son either, because he was a strange and difficult boy, a real patience-wearer if you want to know the truth, and he needed very careful handling, and it is not *natural* for minotaurs to handle things carefully, so it was inevitable that bad things would happen, and the witch had known this, of course she had, the nasty old – ' I look around but there's no one in earshot – 'the nasty old *bitch*. Yes. The bitch. And she was enjoying herself very much, watching on her nasty old plasma screen, smoking her nasty old drugs, and on the subject of drugs, Carl used to be a heroin addict, years ago this was, and the reason he became addicted to heroin was because he was in constant turmoil, being a minotaur in a modern society, and he took the heroin to find inner peace, but the heroin got the better of him and he became addicted, and he stole things in order to pay for all his heroin, TVs and motorbikes and stuff like that, and he got in trouble with the police plenty of times, but it wasn't this that made him stop, it was his wife, who he loved very much, remember, and who was pregnant with his future son, the porcelain son, so he went cold turkey, Carl did, and she brought him thin soup and distracted him with action films while he sweated all the heroin out of his body, and it was very hard for him and he cried out for heroin, and at one point he was almost out the door, but then his wife started crying and so he crawled back into bed with her and put on another film, one with Sylvester Stallone, who has a very high IQ by the way, and the next day he felt better, and he never took heroin ever again, although he did smoke lots of marijuana, but his wife didn't mind this because marijuana grows out of the ground. Which is a flawed logic, I think, but then, she was not perfect. No, she was not perfect.' I turn down Artemis Lane. Close now, very close. '*Anyway*, Carl loved his wife so much that he was often more man than bull, and he did lots of nice things and behaved himself for months at a time, so naturally, the witch got bored watching all this, but she knew there'd be good bits coming up so she kept on watching, and of course, Carl went on to do some *awful* things – like, once, he broke a man's legs because this man said something sexually provocative to his wife, and another time he smashed a beer bottle over a man's head because he called him a bad name, and the bad name was "cunt."' I glance around. 'Cunt, cunt, cunt. Cunty McCunterson Cunterola. Cunt. *Any*way. Another awful thing Carl did, was he pushed his wife over when he was drunk and she landed on her bottom and bruised her coccyx, though this was the only time he ever hurt her, physically anyway, and afterwards he went to anger management class with all the other minotaurs, and it didn't help at all, he was still angry, though he saved up all his anger for the walls and doors of his labyrinth, and it got so full of hoofprints there was more hole than wall, like Swiss cheese, and it's a miracle the whole thing didn't crash to the ground, and his wife, she complained about losing their damage deposit, but really she was just glad that the holes were in the walls and not in her face, and I'm glad of that too.

'And here's the funny thing about his wife – when she eventually left him, it wasn't because he was a minotaur, it was because the spark had gone, which is very sad, but it happens all the time, which is what he said to her – he said, "Babe, we can work at it, we can get it back." And I remember, they were sitting at the kitchen table at the time and the difficult porcelain son with the emerald eyes was eavesdropping near the door – no, that's not strictly true, it was near the light switch, near the fucking light switch, the fucking weirdo, God, he was a right piece of work, but *anyway* … anyway. The wife, Susan was her name, she felt like it would be too much hard work getting the spark back, but she would think about it, and for now, she wanted to be alone, to think about things, and also, she would be taking Sylvester, the difficult porcelain son, because Carl was too much of a bull to handle him and she didn't want him smashed to bits all over the floor, and this was before the nose-smashing incident, remember, so she obviously sensed how volatile the situation could be, because mothers are like that, they have wonderful intuition, and anyway, Carl, he agreed, but said he'd like weekends, and that was fine with Susan, and she left, taking her porcelain son with her, once she got him free from the light switch, that is, which took over half an hour. See? Didn't I tell you he was difficult? And Carl, he got so sad and angry after she left that he became more bull than man, and he drank lots of alcohol, which is really fun by the way, and he got into lots of fights, and then his wife got cancer in her brain, and when he found out, all his anger got swallowed up by sadness, and he took care of her, alongside the NHS, which is wonderful by the way, I don't care what anyone says, and Carl, he brought her home and cleaned her and fed her and, when she got incontinent, he even wiped her bottom, but she grew so ashamed of this that she asked him to get some carers in to do it, so he did, he got the Macmillan nurses in, and they wiped her bottom and administered her diamorphine because she was in lots of pain now and they needed to ease her passing, her death, her fucking death, and Carl watched as they gave her the diamorphine, and isn't it ironic? Because diamorphine is another name for heroin, and their relationship had started with her helping him get off it, and now it was ending with *him* helping *her* get *on* it, and Carl understood the irony and made miserable jokes about it as the nurses connected the drip thingy for the

162

diamorphine, and Susan smiled weakly, and soon she slipped into a diamorphine sleep, and she stayed sleeping for three days with her mouth a small crusty hole, and Dad sat by her side and dabbed her crusty lips with swabs and listened to her breath get slower and raggier, and the porcelain son, well, he was there too, and he just cried himself dry, and he didn't eat a thing and he had nothing to do with light switches for a change, because, obviously, this bad thing was happening, so the light switches hadn't worked anyway, useless waste of fucking time, and then she died, and it was the worst thing in the world. The worst thing in the world. But I'm not going to cry. I'm not going to cry. Dad was there when she 'passed on' – why do they always say it like that? Passed on? As if there's somewhere to pass on to. There isn't, there fucking isn't. Dad was there when she died and became a sack of meat for the worms, let's not get fucking precious, OK? Dad was there but the porcelain boy was not because he'd needed to sleep, what with being up for almost seventy-two hours, so he'd missed it, he'd missed his mum dying, passing, dying, passing, whatever, but he'd come in to see her body, her beautiful sack of meat, and he'd jumped on it like a crazy grieving person and held on tight and didn't let go for hours, and he'd been too frozen with grief to even swat the flies off her cheek and he didn't even care that her body was letting out dead gas, he just held on with his muscles burning and sand pouring down his throat like an hourglass, but I'm not going to cry, I'm *not* going to cry. Because *then*, Carl let some anger back in with the sadness, and he got into *more* fights, and he smashed his son's nose all over the carpet, I swear I'm not going to fucking cry, and it's true that his son was being very difficult, but he shouldn't have smashed his nose all over the carpet. And the son moved out, and a year later, the son moved back in, which is a whole different story, a boring story. And the witch, she'd been really creative with the son – not only was he porcelain, he had a curse on his penis, an evil curse. It was a possessed penis, and it did all the wrong things. It turned to porcelain when it should

163

have been jelly, and it turned to jelly when it should have been porcelain, and it got him in trouble with the minotaur's new girlfriend, who was a sultry duchess from Ely, and it was awful, it was really, really *awful*, and the minotaur went batshit, stamping his hooves in the porcelain boy's bedroom and breathing steam out of his nose, and he charged, he did, he fucking well charged, and he didn't smash the boy, but he did mentally scar him, and that wasn't fair, because it wasn't his fault anyway, it was all down to the witch's evil spell and maybe also the Sultry Duchess of Ely, who was a bit of a flirt. A cock-tease actually. A bloody fucking cock-tease, let's be honest. And anyway, the Sultry Duchess of Ely pleaded with Carl and he coolly listened to her womanly lamentations then pulled out a big gun and shot her in the head and said, '"Consider that a divorce"' in his best ever Schwarzenegger impression and she fell to floor and disappeared in a puff of sexy red smoke, and the next three days the minotaur spent stamping around his labyrinth and getting drunk, and the poor porcelain boy, well, he locked himself in his bedroom and felt very sorry for himself, and he also lost his marbles. Which were made of porcelain.'

I burst out laughing again. There's no one around this time. I clutch my stomach and let out a shrill scream. I don't know why.

'And *then*, on the third day, Carl bashed in his next-door neighbour's head with his big hoof and dragged him into his labyrinth to rot, except he didn't rot, he turned into a fly and flew away, but that's a whole different story.'

One hundred and seventeen.

It should be one hundred and fourteen. That would fit. But look – eleven minus seven equals four. So you can always find a four in there somewhere.

The numbers are shiny smooth copper, or pretend copper. The ones look especially inviting.

I knock the door. Straighten myself out.

Now. Sober Sylvester, he would start panicking now. The second after that knock, he'd get a face like a bowl of knocked over cream. 'What am I doing?' he'd say. But drunk Sylvester, he's a different breed of man. He understands the signals the good doctor has been giving him, and he doesn't question them.

'Drunk Sylvester,' I mutter, staring at the door. 'He's drunk in the street in the morning. Drunk at the door with a hard-on.' Which is a lie – I don't have a hard-on. Not yet.

I knock again.

She's going to open the door in her dressing gown, because it's the weekend and she's relaxing. Watching old black and white films, drinking espresso out of a tiny white cup, her long legs milky-bare, her toes perfect as cock-a-winkles. She'll come to the door and I'll see the shape of her breasts, her lovely soft handfuls of breast, curving out the silk of her dressing gown, yes, silk, and she'll be wearing her glasses, and she'll look like Ava Gardner in a Specsavers advert, and she'll flash one of her rare smiles when she sees me, and she won't be afraid that one of her mentally ill patients has come to her house, because she *wanted* him to come to her house, she made it clear, she let her professionalism drop away like a musky pair of pants, she kicked them off. She'll invite me in and I'll be on her, ripping away the gown, pushing her against the wall, and we'll fuck like mad lions, and I shall be good. *Good*. Definitely better than average. Because I have it in me. Drunk Sylvester has it in him.

I stare at the door.

It's been at least a minute.

'Shit.' I press my forehead against the door. A bit of grit digs into my eyebrow. 'Shitting cunt-hole.'

I want more wine. I'm tired. But I want more wine. I could go to the shop, buy a bottle, and some flowers. Wait on her doorstep. She'll come home with bags of shopping and there I'll be, smiling with handsome emerald eyes over the flowers. Which will be red. Red for sex. And the wine, it'll be the good stuff. I'll get the shopkeeper to show me the good stuff. I'll ask in a theatrical voice, like the Pied Biker, I'll say, 'Show me the good stuff, chappy,' and he will. And we'll drink it, me and Dr Hunter, me and Sheila, we'll drink it, peering at each other over our wine glasses, and then I'll reach out and stroke her nipple with my thumb. Round and round like a dimmer switch.

Except I only have one pound fifty left.

I pull my forehead off the cool wood and stare at the numbers. 117. The first 1 is grubby, the copper coating slightly chipped at the corner. The 7 looks too much like hard work. But the middle 1, it's perfect. Clean and silky smooth. Like Dr Hunter's Mini Milk arms. I reach out and touch it. Cold.

Here's the pattern: I start at the bottom corner and go around the edges, up, across, down, across. I repeat this and then I start spiralling inwards, but of course, it's a rectangular spiralling. I get to the middle and I spiral back out, out, out, to the edges again, and I go round the edges but in reverse order, and then I start again.

It feels like all my pleasure and all my displeasure has been broken up into glass and put into a sack and then I'm shaking the sack, and all the glass bits are clattering into each other, and some bits are sharp and some bits are smooth. My eyes are half-closed. It must look like ecstasy. But it's not a real ecstasy at all. It's coated in glass crumbs.

Around the edges, inwards rectangular spiral, outwards rectangular spiral, back round the edges in reverse, repeat. Repeat, repeat, eyelids sinking, repeat, repeat, repeat, repeat, repeat.

Time disappears. Everything disappears. Though a part of me notices the start of rain. Light spatters.

And then a voice, a male voice:

'Excuse me? Excuse me? Hey. Hey.'

And then a hand on my shoulder, a soft grip. 'Hey.'

And then the grip getting firmer. 'Hey, you. Are you OK, mate?'

And then the grip firmer again, and a pulling, a slight pulling.

I spin around and I punch. I punch the man's face. It just happens, my hand curling up, my fist shooting out. I punch him. A thud. I feel a shudder go all the way up my arm. He steps back, clutching his cheek, spilling envelopes, brown and white envelopes. The postman.

'Fucksake!' he shouts.

'Oh my God, I'm sorry,' I say. 'Oh my God, oh my God.'

He pulls his hand away from his face, looks at it. No blood. I look at his face. No blood. He looks at me. Fifty-ish with greying hair, a thin downturned mouth, dark stubble. Like a sad clown without any make-up on. He glares at me. He has the same look my dad gets when he's about to do something violent.

I run. I jump past him and I run. He tries to grip me but his fingers slip. I run past Pulse 'n' Grain, past the Cardamom Tree, I run like crazy without looking back, my elbows thwapping at my sides, face in a tight grimace, I run and I run and I run.

I'm never touching alcohol again.

The Fourteenth Face

I stop and rest my hands on my thighs. Breathe deep. My jeans are freckled with wet dots, tiny wet dots. Allensbank Road, that's where I am. In the daytime. So that's OK.

Maybe my drunk autopilot legs knew exactly what they were doing when they brought me here. As usual. And they weren't thinking about Patty, who lives ten minutes away. They want nothing to do with her looming misery.

They want the cemetery.

I start walking. Take my legs off autopilot. The rain hasn't got any lighter or heavier. Just a constant, sparse spray. I'm tired and thirsty now, with my thoughts like sewage pumping slowly through a pipe. This is what alcohol does. It's a poison. It told me so itself.

The gates of Cathays Cemetery are large and black with the name in gold writing and various plaques showing opening and closing times and a 'No Dogs' sticker. Because dog muck in a place full of rotting corpses would be unspeakable.

I know where Mum's grave is, even though it's been years. Even though I've never visited. I remember because of the funeral. Me and Dad side by side in suits that didn't fit well, the rest of our family and Mum's family, and all her friends, even the ones who hadn't spoken to her in a long time because she'd married a minotaur who got drunk and smashed things, punched walls, or else skulked around in a dark mood when Mum was trying to host small gatherings. They were there now, these friends, crying with tissues clenched around noses. They spoke to Dad, and some of them were warm, maybe because they'd heard how he'd nursed her till the end, and some of them were cold, maybe because of the times Mum'd rang them up, crying about the brute she'd married, and probably a lot of them thought he used to beat her, which is a natural assumption to make about such a man, but it wasn't true, except that one time with the bruised coccyx. And anyway, they'd all cried, Mum's friends, and Dad had stood there with rigid, hulking shoulders throughout the service, and I didn't look to see if he cried, but he probably did, silently, expressionlessly, just two eyes burning wet and red, maybe a stiffening of the jaw and lips, and anyway, I was too busy with my own crying. And at the end, my great-nan on Mum's side came over in her wheelchair, pushed by a carer from the agency, since there was no one else to push her after great-granddad died, from Hodgkin's lymphoma if you want to know, and my great-nan was called Peggy, short for Margaret, which makes no sense because there's no 'p' in Margaret, it should be Meggy, but once upon a time a person called Margaret decided to become Peggy, and then lots of people copied this, and now it's normal, and that's how this confusing world works, and anyway, Great-Nana Peggy only had one eye – the other had been blown out of her face in World War Two, when she'd been running home from the park during an air raid, and now she had this great fleshy cavity where the eye once lived, only it wasn't grotesque like you'd imagine, it was perfectly smooth and white and clean, and maybe this is why she never hid it under an eyepatch. She came over and she hugged me from her wheelchair with her bony arms, and then she paid her respects to Dad, but coldly and mechanically, her eye filled with disgust and anger and deep sorrow, which is a lot to fit into just one eye. 'It's a terrible thing to bury your grandchild,' she said to Dad, 'but I'm only surprised you didn't put her in her grave much sooner.' She stared at Dad and Dad stared back. He had that look he gets when he's about to let the bull out, and I got

170

frightened, but all he did was snort air out of his nose and walk away. I guess it was this encounter with Great-Nana Peggy that caused him to drink too much at the pub reception. And I believe that if Great-Nana Peggy hadn't gone home five minutes after this graveside encounter on account of her colostomy bag bursting and faeces blossoming on her blouse like a brown flower, at the pub he would have grabbed her and shook her till all her bones broke. So thank God for the brown flower.

It's up by the Whitchurch Road side, Mum's grave. I walk past old-fashioned graves with perched stone angels. I look at the names. Myra and Frederick and Harold and Ivy. Welsh names with Wynns stuck in the middle. A few Greek names ending with 'opolis'. I head up the right path, at least I think it's the right path. It's a confusing cemetery with paths all criss-crossing so you can easily get lost.

It's a nice word, cemetery. Especially when you slow it down. Ssemm-uh-terry. When you give it the time it deserves.

And they're lovely places, cemeteries. Always quiet, always still. I don't know why I don't come to cemeteries more often.

Except I do.

Four years hasn't been enough time.

I get off the path and cut across the grass, which always feels lumpier than it probably is. 'There are never any winners,' I say. 'There are only dead people. Lots of dead people. And satisfied insects.'

It's such a strange and cruel irony that things must feed off death to live.

There are so many headstones, and most have faded writing so you have to stoop and look close. Some have fresh flowers, some have dying flowers, some have none. I finally find Mum's. She has none.

Maybe it's this that makes me burst into immediate tears. She has none. And her headstone is mossy and there are weeds curling up.

I slump down on the damp grass. I should have brought her flowers. There I was, half an hour ago, worrying because I hadn't brought flowers for Dr Hunter, a woman who probably would have rung the police if she'd seen me at her door. I should have brought flowers for my mum.

She always liked things that grew.

I touch the stone and it's cold, bone-cold. I don't want to think about what her face looks like now, down there, so, of course, I think about it. Skin all black and leathery, shrunk to her bones, eyes gone, dust-coloured hair. Limestone teeth, all big without the gums there. The gums eaten by insects and bacteria. A gaunt grin.

The fourteenth face.

'Stop it,' I say, pressing my forehead to the stone. It feels like sacrilege, imagining my mum all rotting like that. But this is the way. Drunk or sober. This is the way.

Beetles crawling through her eye holes.

Maggots in her nose holes.

A restless slime.

'Stop it.' My crying has slown down to a weary sobbing. 'Stop it.'

'So after Carl there was – ' I look at the headstone just over – 'there was Arthur John Andrews. And he was … um, he was…' Oh, for God's sake, stop it, Sylvester, just stop it.

I sit up straight. 'Mum,' I say. 'I'm sorry I didn't visit sooner. I didn't want to. I knew it would be like this.' I wipe my eyes. 'It's not fair. I only want to see your face the way it was when you were OK.' I sniff back snot. Let out a shaky breath. 'Coming here doesn't change anything. That's what I've been afraid of.'

I look at the sky. It's grey. The rain has stopped trying.

I swivel around and press my back against the stone. 'I'm going to remember some nice things right now, just for you.'

And I do. I close my eyes and I remember my mum. Just little snapshots really. Her in the living room, reading a book, I can't remember which book, but let's pretend it was the poetry of

Louise Gluck, which she had on her bookcase. *The Wild Iris*. Her reading that, her brows a little furrowed. Let's not cheapen the memory by trying to make it special. With ethereal sunlight coming through the window and shining off her lovely blonde hair – no, nothing like that. Just reading in her armchair, the radio on in the other room, her hair probably greasy, because she only had a bath twice a week, to save on water. Just reading. And another time, this one with talking bits. Her in the garden, helping me make a snowman. Again, nothing special, not a woman from a shampoo advert spinning around in the snow and laughing out fog through perfect white teeth. Just Mum in Dad's old fleece, smoking a cigarette and standing there, doing a bored smile, saying, 'No, darling, we don't have any coal. Use stones.' Me saying, 'But it's got to be coal!' and her saying: 'It's not the 1950s. Use stones.' And me not understanding what the 1950s had to do with anything, they were just numbers, and then Mum finding me two stones, jagged stones of course, not smooth strokeable stones, and me poking them in the snowface, and her saying, 'Looks like your dad.' Then, later, us going back inside to watch Christmas cartoons. And another one. Not so much a snapshot as a photostory. Mum getting all awkward around me one day when I was twelve, and me not understanding why, and Dad coming into my room later to explain to me in stunted words that 'playing with yourself' is normal, all boys do it, and then me feeling mortified because I suddenly understood Mum's awkwardness – it'd been laundry day and she'd been changing the bedclothes, and obviously she found some sperm, as well as the Page Three girl I'd ripped out of Dad's *Sun* and hidden under my mattress, and then me hiding from her for four whole days, and then finally, her coming up to my room all exasperated, saying, 'For God's sake, Sylvester, it's no big deal, everyone does it. Now come down for dinner and get over it.' And then us being OK, and Mum making silly jokes about farts at the dinner table, which was strange because that wasn't her humour, and in fact she was very embarrassed by farts, but now I can see that she was trying to make light of bodily functions to make me feel OK, and Dad saying, 'Fuck's sake, Susan, don't talk about farts when I'm trying to eat,' and her saying, 'Yes, sir, of course, sir,' or something like that, and then winking at me over her glass of wine. And everything was OK because Mum had fixed it. That's what she did – she fixed everything. Except for me. As if anyone could.

She wasn't perfect. She lost her temper sometimes and shouted at me, and her face would be all twisted like a pink flannel. She ignored me sometimes. Just got fed up of me and acted like I wasn't in the room. And when I was seven and I swore in front of her ('shit', I think it was), she locked me out in the garden all day without food and told me that bad things happen to people who swear, and, of course, this burrowed into my brain and grew roots, very strong roots, which is why I'm so weird about bad language, and I know it's illogical to worry about saying certain words, they're just letters in a sequence, but there are those sturdy twisted roots, thanks to Mum, and why she was so against bad language is an enigma to me, because she wasn't a conservative person, the opposite in fact, so maybe her parents grew the roots in her brain when she was little, or maybe she'd used a swear word one day, 'shit' for example, and it was by pure coincidence just before her family all got wiped out by natural causes and she'd come to the same kind of conclusions that I do about things and got scared that everyone died because of the bad word, who knows, but anyway, it's a shame that I'm so scared to swear because it means I'm repressing stuff, and that is never healthy. Never fucking healthy.

No, she wasn't perfect.

'But you were wonderful,' I say now. 'Best mum ever.' Which is a silly thing to say because I've only ever had one mum, so how would I know? But it's a nice thing to say. Like flowers on a grave.

I lie on the damp grass with my head just touching the headstone. What my mum used to do when she'd been drinking was down two pints of water before going to bed, sleep as long as possible, then down two more as soon as she woke up. She'd eat lots of fatty things throughout the day to soak up the alcohol. Not that there was much alcohol to begin with – she only ever got 'tipsy' – that was her word for it. Which meant smiling a wobbly smile and laughing louder than usual. Not like me today. She would have called that 'totalled', which is what my dad gets from drinking.

Imagine if I got drunk every day? A bottle of wine in the morning before unleashing myself onto the world. I might get into bar fights, like Dad, and smash things over people's heads for saying the wrong word.

'No, probably not,' I tell my mum. 'I don't think I have bull in me. Even though I did punch a postman today. But it could have been worse. I could have punched Dr Hunter. That would have been the worst.'

I stand up. 'Anyway. I'm going now. But I'm going to come back soon with flowers. I don't know what your favourites are, but I'll do my best.'

I lean down and kiss the headstone. 'I love you, Mum. Rest in peace.'

A flash of her rotting skull.

Don't indulge it.

I'll go back to Patty's, I think. She might be out of her Annie Wilkes mood now. I can talk to her about what happened with Aled and she can give me advice, solid advice. And then I can drink lots of water, then sleep, then drink lots of water. And once I've flushed all the poison out of my body I can think about things clearly. And maybe I will be so mortified by the memories of this drunken spree that I will want to kill myself, but I won't kill myself, I'll just get through it.

I pass the polluted angels and mossy crosses. I leave through the gates and turn right. And there is a man in front of me. Fleece jacket done up to the chin, mouth a grim slit. Hulking shoulders.

'Sylv?' he says. He's got flowers in his hand, yellow flowers.

It's this that stops me running. Flowers for Mum.

'"Hello, cutie pie,"' he says, doing Schwarzenegger. '"One of us is in deep trouble."' And I can tell that he regrets saying this as soon as it's out of his mouth. Now is not the time for these games.

'Dad,' I say.

'You came,' he says.

'What?'

'Finally ready to face it?'

My eyes grow as wide as apples. The anniversary! Mum's anniversary. Four years today. 'Oh wow,' I say. 'Actually I forgot. But I came anyway.'

Dad taps the side of his head. 'Your subconscious.'

But it feels like more than that. It feels like magic. I imagine the witch watching through her plasma screen. Waiting for the good stuff. Getting bored round about now because me and Dad aren't trying to kill each other.

'You look like shit,' he says. 'Where've you been?'

'Nowhere,' I say. Which is stupid.

He looks at the cemetery gates a while, thinking. He's clean-shaven and his eyes are bright. Sober. 'I was worried,' he says, looking down at the flowers.

'Well,' I say.

He taps the flowers against his palm. 'You shouldn't have run off like that.'

'You shouldn't have done some things too,' I say.

He raises his free hand in admission. 'I know. I'm just saying. I was worried about you.' He runs his big hand up the plastic covering the flower stems. 'So where'd you go?'

I shake my head. 'I went to a party. I got drunk.'

He smiles. 'You? Drunk?'

I nod.

'What did you drink?'

'Wine. Red wine. Rioja.'

Another smile. 'It's pronounced *ree-o-cha*.'

'Ree-o-cha,' I say, testing it.

'What did it taste like?'

'Horrible.'

He nods. 'It usually does.' He gestures toward the gates with the flowers. 'Wanna go and visit your mum?'

'I already have.'

'Come and sit on that bench with me a bit.' He walks through the gates and up the path before I can respond. But I follow. Of course I follow. Because he has flowers for Mum and bright, sad, sober eyes. He sits on one end of the bench. Places the flowers on his lap, looks around. I sit on the other end.

'She liked these, she did, your mum,' he says, waggling the flowers.

'What are they?'

'Carnations. They were her favourite. And daffodils.' He looks at me. 'She had them in the hospital room when you were born. She liked dandelions too. She liked weeds as much as flowers. She made dandelion wine once. Horrible.'

I nod.

'You need a good sleep,' he says. 'You OK?'

I shrug. 'Tired.'

He nods. 'A good sleep. That's what you need. And two pints of water, then two more pints when you wake up, then a dirty sarnie. Like your mum used to.'

'Like Mum used to,' I say, nodding.

There's a long silence. Dad looks around, jaw set. He takes a long breath through his nose. 'I shouldn't have went for you like I did.'

'No,' I say.

'Are you gonna move out again?'

'I don't know.' I squeeze my knees together. 'What happened with Aled? Did you – did you…' I can't finish the sentence.

'Kill him?' he says. 'Nah. Just knocked him out.'

'What's going to happen now?'

He does a wry smile. 'Well. Nothing. Hopefully.'

'What do you mean? What happened?'

'Well. I knocked him out, he came to, then we had a little chat.'

'Did he call the police on you?'

'No. I'm hoping he won't.' He looks down at the flowers. Pulls a petal out, drops it, watches it float to the ground. 'I threatened him.'

I stare at him, mouth open.

'I was backed into a corner. Beastly old Dad. But you know what else I did? To square things up? I promised him I'd move out. I said, "Aled, in six weeks I'll be gone. And you will be rid of me forever."'

'Did you mean it?'

He thinks about it, scrunching his lips. 'Probably not. I was just thinking the other day that I'd like to decorate. Lick of paint on the walls, new sofa maybe. I'll get you some of those handclap lights. Or the glitter. The glitter's fine.'

He looks down at the flowers. 'I haven't been happy since your mum passed.' I imagine the flowers turning into a pale-yellow prism behind his wet eyes. 'And even when I was with her, I don't think I was happy. But I was happ*ier*.'

'I'm sorry I got – you know, around your girlfriend,' I say.

He shrugs. 'It happens.'

'It happens to me all the time,' I say.

'It'll pass. You're young.'

We go silent again. He rubs his eyes with a fist. 'You know what else I did for Aled?' he says.

'What?'

'I made him an ice pack. Out of some peas.' He clears his throat. 'I said to him, I said, "Aled, give peas a chance."' He looks at me expectantly, his eyes wrinkling. And he laughs. But I don't join in.

He reaches across the space between us and ruffles my hair. 'Always so sensitive, aren't you?'

178

I'm too tired to flinch.

'Remember when you were little, and you made that false eye for your great-grandmother out of a conker?'

'No.'

He smiles. 'You were only about four. I took you conker picking, remember? That time down the woods?'

'No.'

'You found the roundest conker and you said, "I'm going to make this into an eye for Great-Nana Peggy." And you took it home and your mum got you some acrylic paints, and you painted it white, and then you did the iris. You took such care with it. Like a little Picasso. And then you let it dry near the radiator. And when she next came round, your bitch of a great-grandmother, may she rest in peace, you gave it to her and said, "Now you'll be able to see better." And Peggy, she didn't know what to say. But she took it and she thanked you, and she popped it in her socket, and she made this big fuss about how she could see things in 20/20 now, and you were over the moon.'

I smile. 'I don't remember any of that.'

'She wore it every time she came over for the next year or so. She was a cunt, your great-grandmother, but she did that for you.'

'That was nice of her.'

He does a reluctant snort of acknowledgement.

There is a silence that lasts half a minute.

'Tell me something, Dad,' I say, eventually. '"What is best in life?"'

'"To crush your enemies and drive them before you and to hear da lamentations of da women."' He smiles. Takes a cigarette pack out of his pocket and lights one. 'Hey, Sylv. "Drop dead."'

'"I don't do requests."'

'You're getting better at that,' he says. 'Still not as good as your Van Damm though.'

I point at his cigarette. '"It's bad for your health you know,"' I say, doing Stallone from *Cobra*.

179

Dad's eyes squint through his cigarette smoke. '"What is, pinche?"' His accent is exaggerated Mexican.

I pluck the cigarette from his mouth, my fingers skimming his lips. '"Me."'

He lets out a laugh and it turns into a deep cough. I hand him back the cigarette. He takes a long drag and bizarrely it stops the coughing. He says, '"Let me tell you something you already know. The world ain't all sunshine and rainbows."' This is Rocky giving his son a motivational speech in *Rocky Balboa*. '"It's a very mean and nasty place, and I don't care how tough you are, it will beat you to your knees and keep you there permanently if you let it."' The cough hasn't quite left his voice and he sounds husky, more Stallone than ever. '"You, me, or nobody is gonna hit as hard as life,"' he continues. '"But it ain't about how hard you hit. It's about how hard you can get hit and keep moving forward; how much you can take and keep moving forward."' He pauses, cigarette in his mouth, trying to remember the rest. His bright blue eyes are watering from the smoke. 'Oh, I remember. "I'm always gonna love you, no matter what. No matter what happens. You're my son and you're my blood. You're the best thing in my life. But until you start believing in yourself, you ain't gonna have a life."' He does a strange thin-lipped smile and says, in his normal voice, 'You remember the last line?'

'"Don't forget to visit your mother."'

He nods. 'Funny, that.'

There is another silence. The longest yet. And then Dad taps the yellow flowers on his knee and says, 'Right then. Wanna go and visit your mother? Together? She'd like that.'

And she would.

I imagine her ratty skull creaking into a grin. It's not a nice thing to think. But at least I made her smile.

ABOUT HONNO

Honno Welsh Women's Press was set up in 1986 by a group of women who felt strongly that women in Wales needed wider opportunities to see their writing in print and to become involved in the publishing process. Our aim is to develop the writing talents of women in Wales, give them new and exciting opportunities to see their work published and often to give them their first 'break' as a writer. Honno is registered as a community co-operative. Any profit that Honno makes is invested in the publishing programme. Women from Wales and around the world have expressed their support for Honno. Each supporter has a vote at the Annual General Meeting. For more information and to buy our publications, please write to Honno at the address below, or visit our website: www.honno.co.uk

Honno, 14 Creative Units, Aberystwyth Arts Centre
Aberystwyth, Ceredigion SY23 3GL

Honno Friends

We are very grateful for the support of the Honno Friends: Jane Aaron, Annette Ecuyere, Audrey Jones, Gwyneth Tyson Roberts, Beryl Roberts, Jenny Sabine.

For more information on how you can become a Honno Friend, see: http://www.honno.co.uk/friends.php